Oliver Doyle

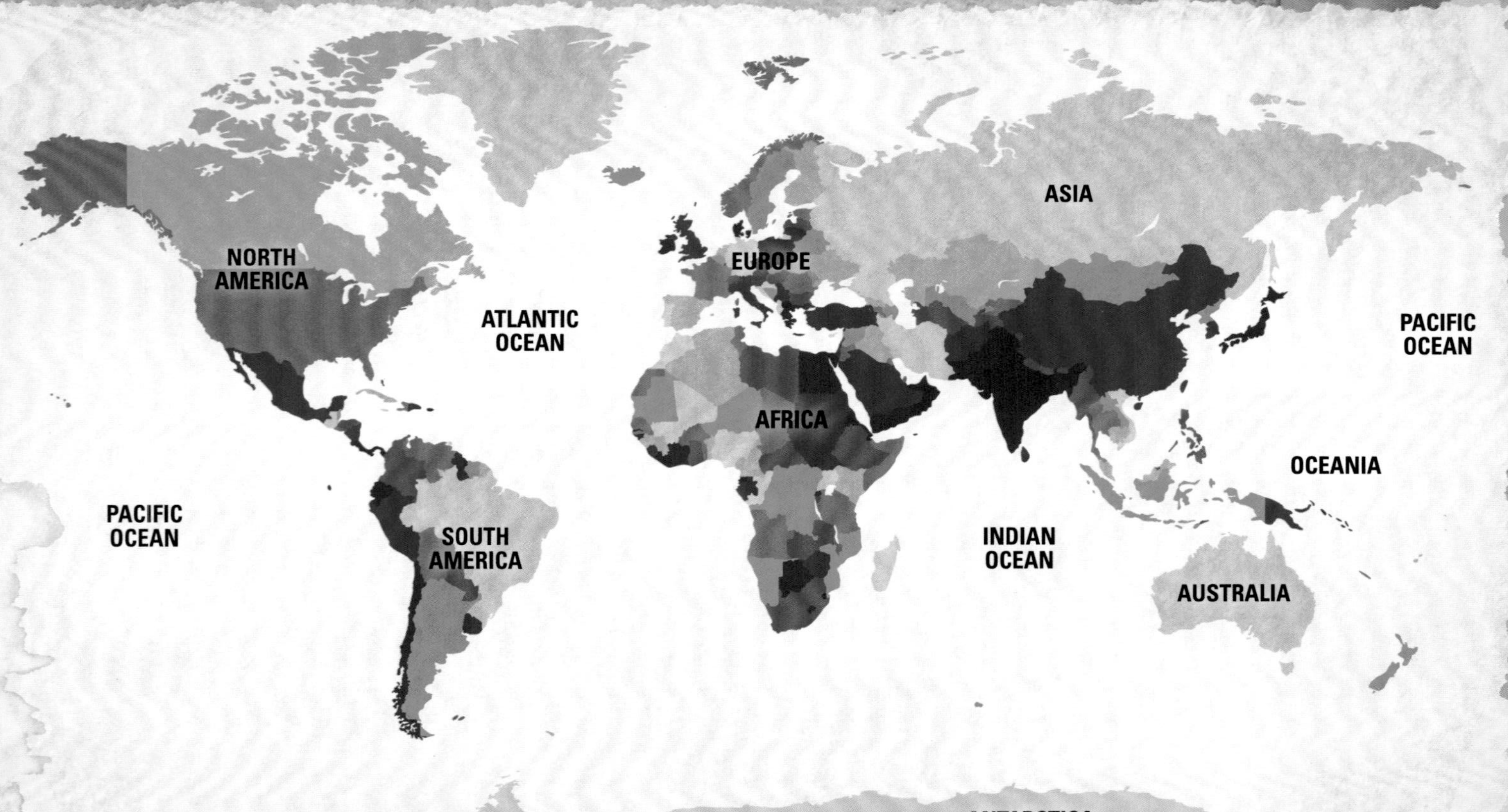
NORTH AMERICA
ATLANTIC OCEAN
EUROPE
ASIA
PACIFIC OCEAN
AFRICA
OCEANIA
PACIFIC OCEAN
SOUTH AMERICA
INDIAN OCEAN
AUSTRALIA
ANTARCTICA

CONTENTS

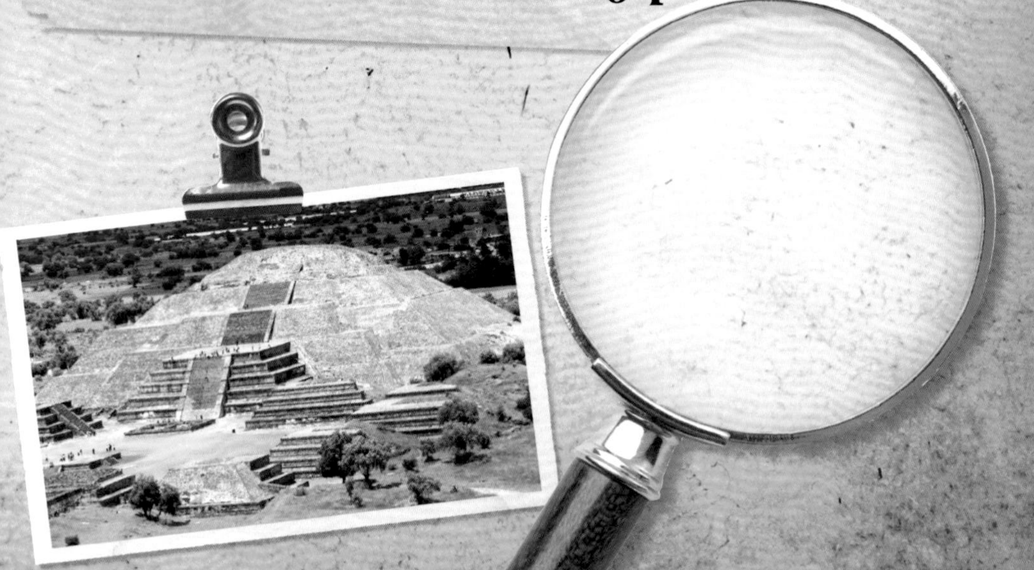

CHAPTER 1

BIGFOOT AND OTHER

Our fascination with strange mysteries of marvelous monsters dates from ancient times. The creatures in this book are all CRYPTIDS. This means they are legendary—there is no scientific proof they exist and eyewitness reports can't be trusted. But what do you think? Read on and examine the evidence!

WILD MAN OF THE WOODS

In 1793, European settlers in North America reported sightings of a "hairy ape man." A legend soon grew of a "wild man of the woods." During the 1800s and early 1900s, newspapers reported scary stories of hunters and trappers and their terrifying encounters with Sasquatches, hairy apelike men.

BATTLE OF APE CANYON

In July 1924, an Oregon newspaper ran a story about gold miners in the Mount St. Helens region who came under attack from a group of Sasquatches. While fetching water, the men saw a creature watching them from behind a tree. It stood over 6.5 feet (2 m) tall. At night, three Sasquatches attacked the men's cabin. They pounded the walls with large rocks and two of them climbed onto the roof. By morning, however, the creatures had vanished.

MONSTERS

STOLEN AWAY

Another strange event was reported one summer's night in 1924. While camping in the mountains of British Columbia, Albert Ostman claimed he was carried off by four hairy, apelike people. They held him prisoner for several days. Eventually he managed to escape by distracting them with a gold box!

EXAMINING THE EVIDENCE

Sasquatch

For centuries, Native American people have told stories of Bigfoot, or Sasquatch. This monster takes the form of a massive HUMANOID creature covered in fur who lives in remote forested areas. Many people claim to have seen Bigfoot—but do these tales prove he's really out there?

BIGFOOT SIGHTINGS

During the 1900s, more and more people came forward with stories of Bigfoot sightings and the legend continued to grow. Armed with the new technology of photography, the cryptid hunters now had equipment that might provide concrete evidence that monsters were among us!

BIG FEET

In 1928, Muchalat Harry, a fur trapper from Vancouver Island in British Columbia, claimed he was carried off at night by a huge male Sasquatch. The creature took him to a camp of around 20 other monsters. Seeing piles of gnawed bones lying around, Harry was terrified he would be eaten, but luckily escaped to tell his tale.

CONTINUE

STRANGE STORIES

William Roe's account

Roe was a hunter and trapper living in Alberta, Canada. In October 1955, he was approaching an abandoned mine when he saw what he took to be a grizzly bear in the bushes. When the creature emerged, Roe saw it was a giant, hairy man. It squatted and began eating leaves off a bush before catching Roe's scent and looking at him. Standing up, it began to walk away rapidly. Roe raised his rifle, but the creature looked him in the eyes. Suddenly, Roe changed his mind and held his fire.

Real or HOAX? The blurry photo of Bigfoot, below, was taken by a backpacker on November 17, 2005, in the mountains of southern Washington state.

► RUBY CREEK INCIDENT

George and Jennie Chapman and their three children lived near the village of Ruby Creek in British Columbia. In the summer of 1941, while George was away working, Jennie and her eldest son spotted a gigantic hairy man near their home. The creature cried out and began striding toward them. Alarmed, they fled back to the house.

BIGFOOT

HITTING THE

Modern interest in Bigfoot took off in 1958, sparked by unusual events at Bluff Creek in northern California. On August 27, a construction crew building a road turned up for work to discover some strange footprints in the soil. They looked like the footprints of a gigantic human.

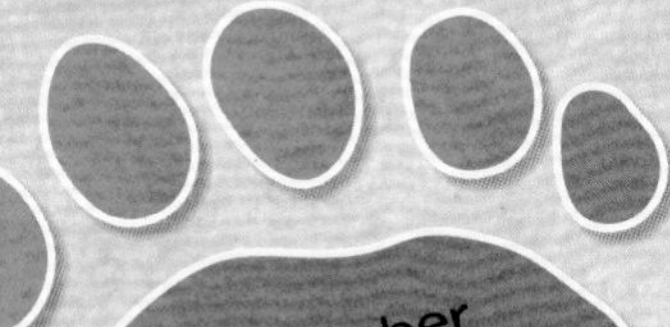

In October 1966, the Corey family was visited by a 7-foot-tall (2 m) Sasquatch, which they said killed the family dog. There were many similar reports around the same time in California.

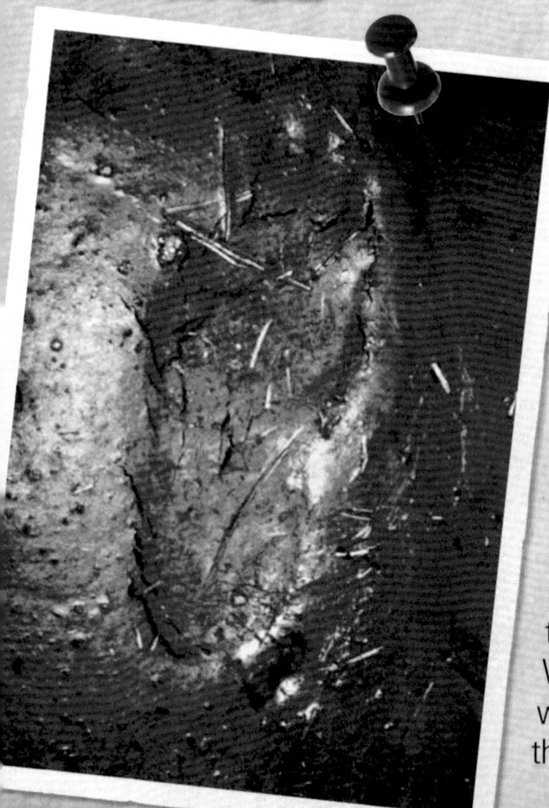

◄ FOOTPRINTS

Bulldozer operator Jerry Crew discovered the prints. He made a plaster of Paris CAST of one of them and was photographed with it for the local newspaper. The story was taken up by newspapers across the United States and the world. Several CRYPTOZOOLOGISTS (people who study cryptids) visited the site, made more casts, and recorded eyewitness reports of encounters. Later it emerged that the head of the construction firm, Ray Wallace, owned a pair of gigantic wooden feet and had faked many of the Bigfoot prints!

HEADLINES

◄ REPORTS MULTIPLY

After the Bluff Creek episode, stories of Bigfoot encounters came flooding in. In 1959, a woman camping in British Columbia was startled by a humanlike ape watching her from behind some trees. In 1961, a man was chased by a Sasquatch in the hills above Alpine, Oregon. In June 1963, another man reported seeing a female Sasquatch with a baby catching fish near Yale, in Washington state.

EXAMINING THE EVIDENCE

Did Ray Wallace fake all the Bluff Creek footprints?

SKEPTICS believe that practical joker Wallace faked all the footprints at Bluff Creek, including the originals found by Jerry Crew. They say Wallace's company was falling behind with its work and Wallace needed a reason to extend the deadline. However, Wallace was away on business when some of the tracks appeared. Believers in the Sasquatch say that Wallace took to hoaxing after the first prints appeared, so that he could exploit the story.

BIGFOOT CAUGHT ON

In 1967, Roger Patterson shot a short film of a mysterious creature at Bluff Creek, in northern California. This is the most important piece of evidence for the existence of Bigfoot. But is the film real, or a gigantic hoax?

The oldest stories about Sasquatch are told by North American native peoples. The name of the creature varies from one tribe to another. The Micmac call it "Chenoo," the Penobscot know it as "Kiwakwe," while the Cherokee call it "Chickly Cudly."

▼ PATTERSON'S STORY

In October 1967, Roger Patterson and his friend Bob Gimlin headed into the wilderness in search of Sasquatch. After some hours they reached a creek running through a canyon. Beside the creek, about 25 feet (8 m) away, they saw a creature. It spotted them and began to walk off. Patterson grabbed his camera and ran after it. He tripped and fell but kept filming. The creature turned to look at him, then rounded a bend and disappeared from sight.

CAMERA

► SASQUATCH SPOTTING

Since 1967, other Sasquatch films have come to light, but none match the quality of the original Patterson film. They include the Freeman footage, shot in 1994 by forestry worker Paul Freeman in Washington state. This shows a hairy humanlike figure crossing a path and disappearing into the woods. The Redwoods footage (1995), filmed on a rainy night in northern California, shows a creature moving slowly in the beam of an automobile's headlights. The Manitoba footage (2005) shows a strange figure on the banks of the Nelson River.

EXAMINING THE EVIDENCE

Truth or dare?

Some people think the Patterson film is a fake. They say it shows a creature who looks like a human in a costume. But some biologists say that for such a creature to walk upright, it would need an extended heel and the Bigfoot in the film has one of these. And there is no evidence to show that trick effects had been used by the filmmakers.

THE SKUNK

In the 1960s, Florida police received reports that an apelike creature was living in the state's swamplands. It sounded like Bigfoot, except for one distinguishing feature. It smelled like a mix of rotten eggs and manure. One witness said it stank like a skunk that had rolled around in a garbage truck! It became known as the Skunk Ape.

FOUL ODOR

In 1966, a Florida woman reported being chased into her house by an apelike creature with a round head and long arms. In July that year, a man came across a hairy human in the forests bordering the Anclote River. He said it had a rancid, putrid odor. Sightings continued through the 1980s and 1990s. In 2000, a group of tourists saw a large, apelike animal moving around in a swamp. Later it was seen crossing the road near the house of a local fire chief. One man took a photograph (right) of the beast as it retreated into the swampland.

APE

In 1979, workmen sent to demolish a remote farmstead near Ochopee, Florida, noticed a foul smell coming from the cellar. They assumed an animal had died until one of the men saw a creature climb out of the cellar and walk away.

JENNIFER WARD

In 2004, Jennifer Ward was driving home when something at the roadside caught her attention. It was a tall, hairy creature, standing on two legs. Ward said the area around the animal's eyes was whitish, and its lips were the color and texture of a dog's paw pad. This fit with other people's descriptions of the Skunk Ape. The image, right, shows an artist's impression of Ward's encounter.

THE YETI

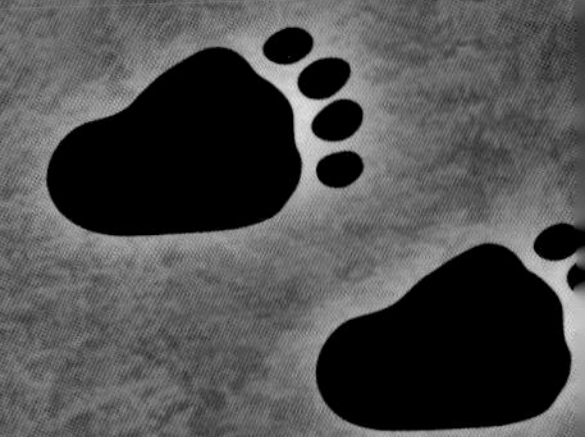

In 1921, British climbers on Mount Everest saw dark figures moving in a snowfield above them. When they reached the snowfield, the climbers found large, humanlike footprints. Their Sherpa guides said the prints had been made by *Metoh-Kangmi*, which translates as "Abominable Snowman," also known as Yeti.

A TAILLESS ANIMAL

In 1976, six forestry workers came across a strange, tailless animal covered in reddish-brown fur. They obtained some hair samples, which were studied but could not be identified.

EYEWITNESS TO MYSTERY

Hairy man

A Chinese farmer describes an encounter with a Yeti: "In the summer of 1977, I went to Dadi Valley to cut logs. Between 11 A.M. and noon, I ran into the 'hairy man' in the woods. It came closer and I got scared so I retreated until my back was against a stone cliff . . . I raised my ax, ready to fight for my life. We stood like that, neither of us moving for a long time. Then I groped for a stone and threw it at him. It hit his chest. He uttered several howls and rubbed the spot . . . Then he turned . . . and leaned against a tree, then walked away . . ."

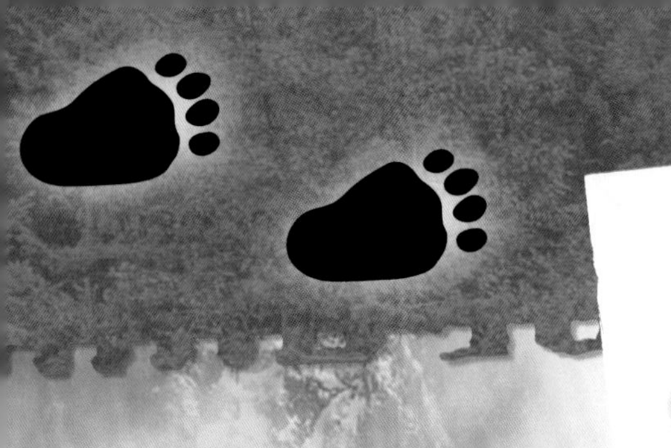

FOOTPRINTS IN THE SNOW

In 1951, Everest mountaineers Eric Shipton and Michael Ward found footprints that may have been made by a Yeti. Sir Edmund Hillary and Sherpa Tenzing Norgay also encountered strange footprints on their celebrated climb to the summit of Mount Everest in 1953.

MOUNTAIN MYSTERY

In 1925, N. A. Tombazi, a Greek photographer, was on an expedition in the Himalayas when he and his guides caught sight of a humanlike figure in the distance. The creature soon departed, but again left strange footprints in the snow.

THE BIG

It is said that on the mountain of Ben MacDhui in the Scottish Highlands there lurks a huge, terrifying creature.The Scots call it *Am Fear Liath Mor,* or the Big Gray Man. It has been described as an old figure in robes, a giant, and even a devil. The Big Gray Man strikes fear and panic in anyone who comes near it.

Scientists have suggested that the Big Gray Man may be a HALLUCINATION caused by isolation or exhaustion. Either way, you wouldn't want to be wandering the mountains alone!

FOOTSTEPS

In 1891, Norman Collie was descending through mist from the peak of Ben MacDhui when he heard footsteps behind him. At first, he assumed it was the echo of his own steps, but the noises did not match his movements. They sounded as though a giant was following him. Terrified, Collie ran blindly for 5 miles (8 km) down the mountain until he could no longer hear the noise.

GRAY MAN

FOREST CHASE

In the 1990s, three men were walking in a forest near the mountain when they spotted a humanlike figure running on the track a little way ahead of them. A few weeks later, the men were driving in the area when they realized they were being followed by the same creature. It kept pace with their car, even at speeds of 45 miles per hour (72 km/h), before eventually disappearing.

FACT HUNTER

Brocken specter

A brocken specter is an optical illusion seen on a misty mountainside or in a cloud bank when the sun is low. When a person's shadow is cast onto low-lying clouds opposite the sun, it makes it seem as though there is a large, shadowy human figure there.

LOCH NESS

One of the most famous of all mythical beasts is the LOCH Ness monster. Loch Ness is a lake in Scotland. In AD 565, Saint Columba was the first person to record having seen a monster in the loch. But Nessie mania only really took off in the 1900s.

Loch Ness is 24 miles (38 km) long and, in places, 1,000 feet (304 km) deep, so there's plenty of space for a huge monster to hide! Urquhart Castle (below) overlooks the loch.

SOMETHING IN THE WATER

In April 1933, a local couple saw an enormous beast rolling and playing in the water. Then a fisherman saw what he described as a long-necked creature, around 30 feet (9 m) in length, with a serpent's head. Later that year, a family from London encountered a massive, long-necked animal that strolled across their path and then disappeared into the water.

MONSTER

► FAMOUS PHOTO

There have been many attempts to capture Nessie on film. One of the most famous photographs, showing the monster's head and neck, was published in 1934. It was later revealed to be a fake. Nonetheless, the sightings continued. In June 1993, a couple saw a 40-foot-long (12 m) creature with a giraffelike neck in the waters of the loch.

EXAMINING THE EVIDENCE

A neck like a conger eel

In May 2001, at around 6 A.M., James Gray was fishing on Loch Ness, when he spotted something strange: "Soon, it was about 6 feet (1.8 m) out of the water but seconds later it had become a black kind of blob as it disappeared. It had curled forward and gone down . . . This was certainly no seal. It had a long black neck almost like a conger eel, but I couldn't see a head. It didn't seem to bend very much but as it went under, it sort of arched and disappeared."

THE HUNT

The search for Nessie continues to this day. In 1987, scientists carried out Operation Deepscan, a SONAR sweep of the loch. Deepscan didn't find the monster, but reported various hard-to-explain sonar echoes in the extreme depths.

NESSIE'S LAIR

Recent sonar explorations have revealed huge underwater caverns near the bottom of Loch Ness. These have been nicknamed Nessie's Lair. Some scientists suggest they may be big enough to hide a family of creatures. If the monster does exist, a breeding colony would be necessary for its survival.

FACT HUNTER

Lake monster

A lake monster is a large freshwater-dwelling animal that is the subject of MYTHOLOGY, rumor, or local folklore but whose existence lacks scientific support. Nessie is one of the most famous lake monsters. Most scientists believe lake monsters are hoaxes, or misinterpretations of known and natural phenomena. Things that could be mistaken for monsters include seals, otters, deer, diving water birds, large fish, logs, mirages, or unusual wave patterns.

▼ COULD NESSIE BE A PLESIOSAUR?

Some experts say Nessie bears a strong resemblance to a creature now thought to be extinct: the plesiosaur, a marine reptile not found on Earth for over 60 million years. Plesiosaurs had large flippers, a small head, and a large body. Sometimes they are described as "snakes threaded through the bodies of turtles." A few of these animals may have been stranded in the loch after the Ice Age. But the plesiosaur was probably cold-blooded, so it is unlikely that it would have survived the chilly conditions of a Scottish lake.

STRANGE NOISES

In March 2000, a team of Norwegian scientists picked up bizarre grunting and snorting noises in the water. They sounded similar to noises recorded in a Norwegian lake that also has a monster legend attached to it.

Okanagan Lake is in British Columbia, Canada. It is around 100 miles (160 km) long and up to 984 feet (300 m) deep. The native Salish tribe believed a terrible serpent, which they called *N'ha-a-itk*, or the "Lake Demon," lurked in its depths. They said the beast had a cave dwelling near the middle of the lake, and they would make sacrifices to please the monster.

THE MODERN LEGEND

European settlers initially scoffed at the legend. But over the years the Ogopogo, as it came to be known, began to be taken seriously. European immigrants started seeing strange phenomena in the lake during the mid-1800s. One story told of a man crossing the lake with his two tethered horses swimming behind. Some strange force pulled the animals under, and the man only managed to save himself by cutting them loose.

SIGHTINGS

Most alleged sightings have occurred around the city of Kelowna, on the eastern shore of the lake. Witnesses say the creature is up to 50 feet (15 m) long, with green skin, several humps, and a huge, horselike head.

Other lake monsters of the world include Auli (Lake Chad, Africa), Brosno Dragon (Brosno Lake, Russia), and Bessie (Lake Erie, Ohio). A $100,000 reward has been offered for the capture of Nessie.

EXAMINING THE EVIDENCE

What could it be?

British cryptozoologist Karl Shuker has categorized the Ogopogo as a "many hump" type of lake monster. He says it could be a primitive serpentine whale such as Basilosaurus. However, skeptics say the sightings are misidentifications of common animals such as otters, beavers, lake sturgeon, or objects such as floating logs.

MOVIE MONSTER

The Ogopogo was allegedly caught on film in 1968, as a dark object propelling itself through shallow water near the shore. Another film, in 1989, showed a snakelike animal flicking its tail. The Ogopogo (below) seems like a more aggressive cousin of the Loch Ness monster.

THE LUSCA

Around the Bahamas and the southeastern coast of the United States there are tales of a giant octopus that captures unwary swimmers and small boats. The people of the islands call it the Lusca and believe it lives in deep underwater caves.

MYSTERIOUS CARCASS

In November 1896, two men were cycling along the Florida coast when they spotted a huge, silvery pink carcass on the beach. It was 23 feet (7 m) long, 18 feet (5.5 m) wide, and seemed to have multiple legs. It weighed 7–8 tons (6–7 t). The men informed a local scientist, who examined the corpse and declared it was some kind of octopus. But other experts said it was probably just the head of a sperm whale. Tests carried out in 1971 and 1986 seemed to confirm that it was indeed part of a gigantic octopus. But even more detailed tests in 1995 suggested that the carcass was indeed part of a whale.

RECORD BREAKER

Scientists suggest that the Lusca may be a giant squid, which has been known to grow to very large sizes. The largest squid on record is a female giant squid that washed ashore on a New Zealand beach in 1887. It was 59 feet (18 m) long and weighed 1 ton (0.9 t).

GIANT OCTOPUS

Various accounts say the Lusca can grow to between 75 feet (23 m) and 200 feet (60 m) in length. No octopus approaching that size has ever been found. However, on January 18, 2011, the body of what appeared to be a giant octopus washed ashore in the Bahamas. According to eyewitness reports, the remains represented only a portion of the head and mouthparts of the original creature. Local fishermen estimate the total length of the creature to have been between 20 and 30 feet (6 and 9 m).

THE MONGOLIAN

In the sand dunes of the Gobi Desert is said to lurk a creature so feared by the Mongolian people that they are scared even to speak its name. When they do, they call it the *Allghoi Khorkhoi*, or "large intestine worm," because this fat, red, deadly snakelike monster looks similar to a cow's intestines. In the West, the monster is known as the Mongolian death worm.

DEATH FROM A DISTANCE

The death worm can kill people instantly. Some believe it spits a lethal toxin. Others say it emits a massive electrical charge. Mongolian nomads believe the giant worm covers its prey with an acidic venom so powerful it can corrode metal. Legend says that when the creature attacks, it raises half its body out of the sand and starts to inflate until it squirts a shower of lethal poison over its victim. The poison is so powerful that the prey dies instantly.

DEATH WORM

STRANGE STORIES

The Minhocão

Another legendary wormlike creature is the Minhocão, of southern Brazil. This monster is said to live at river crossings, where witnesses claim to have seen it drag livestock under the water. According to an account from 1877, the Minhocão makes trenches big enough to divert rivers and overturn trees. The giant worm has scaly black skin "as thick as pine tree bark," a piglike snout, and two tentacle-like structures protruding from its head.

WHAT IS IT?

According to legend, the death worm measures up to 5 feet (1.5 m) in length. Experts are certain it is not a real worm because the Gobi Desert is too hot for worms to survive. The most probable explanation is that the death worm is a type of venomous snake. This magnified image, right, shows a parasitic tapeworm, which lives in the human gut. Could the Mongolian death worm be related to this real-life monster?

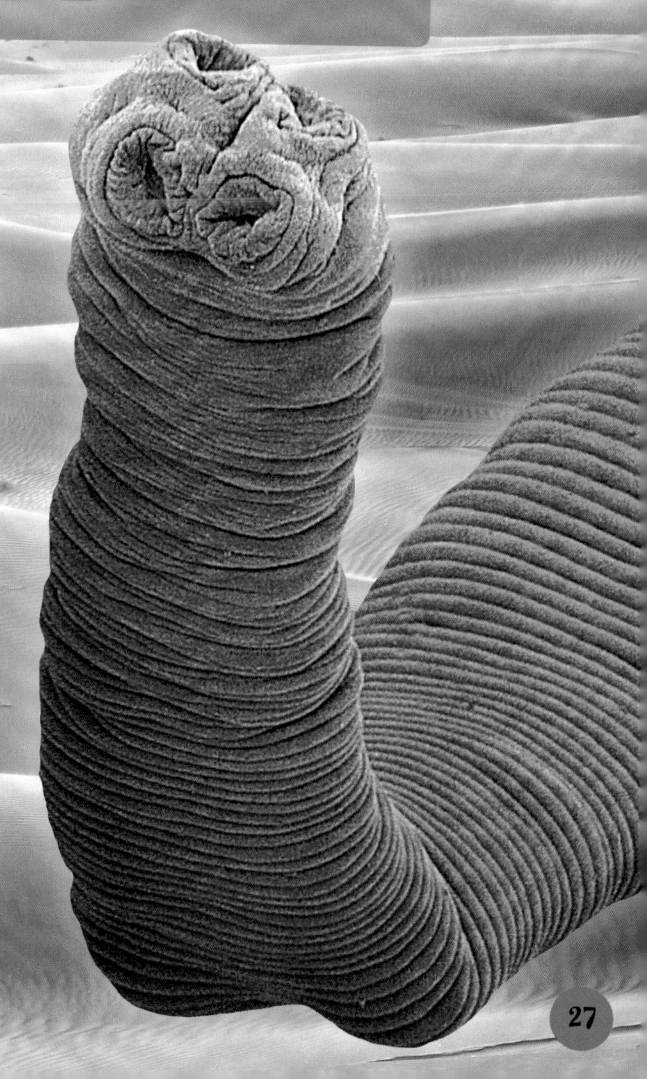

MOTHMAN

In 1966, sightings of a huge, strange "bird" were reported around Point Pleasant, West Virginia. Five gravediggers preparing a plot said they saw a "brown human being" take to the air from nearby trees and fly over their heads. The creature came to be known as Mothman.

FLYING MONSTER

On November 15, 1966, two young couples were driving in an area near Point Pleasant. As they passed an old generator plant, they saw that its door appeared to have been ripped off. Then they saw two red eyes shining out of the gloom. The eyes belonged to a man-shaped creature over 7 feet (2 m) tall, with wings folded against its back. As the creature approached, the young people ran away. Glancing back, they saw it take to the air and rise straight up without flapping its wings. It had a 10 foot (3 m) wingspan and kept pace with their car despite the vehicle's high speed. The creature disappeared before they reached Point Pleasant.

EYEWITNESS TO MYSTERY

Terrible glowing eyes

On November 16, 1966, a young mother was driving to a friend's house just outside Point Pleasant when she saw a strange red light in the sky. Arriving at her destination, she heard something rustling near her car. She recalled, "It rose up slowly from the ground. A big gray thing. Bigger than a man, with terrible, glowing eyes." As she fled into the house, the creature followed and stared in through the windows. The police were called, but by the time they arrived, the creature had disappeared.

BRIDGE DISASTER

In 1967, Mothman was seen by many witnesses, including firemen and pilots. Then, on December 15, the Silver Bridge linking Point Pleasant to Ohio suddenly collapsed, causing the deaths of 46 people. Mothman was rarely seen after that. Some people believe the bridge disaster may have been the monster's terrible final act.

CHAPTER 2

ALIEN ENCOUNTERS

Are we alone in the universe, or does evidence exist of alien life out there? Have people from other planets already visited Earth? Over the years, many people claim to have seen mysterious flying objects. Is there an obvious explanation for these alien encounters, or are they just tall tales?

GHOST FLIERS

So-called "ghost fliers" were spotted several times over Scandinavia between 1932 and 1937. They took the form of huge aircraft, much bigger than anything in existence at the time. At night, they shined dazzlingly bright searchlights onto the ground. Eyewitnesses reported that they performed aerobatics and achieved speeds impossible for any known aircraft.

FOO FIGHTERS

During World War II, strange glowing balls about 3 feet (1 m) across, known as "foo fighters," were seen by pilots over Europe. The foo fighters flew alongside bomber formations for minutes at a time before either disappearing or flying off at high speed. Pilots assumed they were some form of enemy weapon and tried to shoot them down—without success.

EXAMINING THE EVIDENCE

Are UFOs real?

People who say they have seen UFOs are probably telling the truth, but could their senses have been deceiving them? Some UFO reports have been explained by flights of secret aircraft, weapons, and weather balloons, or by light phenomena such as mirages and searchlights. Others could have been prompted by the misidentification of clouds, planets, bright stars, METEORS, artificial satellites, or the moon. Others have been deliberate hoaxes.

THE "FIRST"

On the morning of June 24, 1947, Kenneth Arnold set off from Chehalis, Washington, to his home in Oregon in his single-engine light aircraft. While flying over Mount Rainier, he saw something that would change his life and begin a new era.

FLASH OF LIGHT

Arnold described a bright flash of light sweeping over his plane. He thought it was the sun reflecting off a nearby aircraft. Then, far to the north, he saw a line of nine aircraft flying toward him at an angle. Each aircraft was shaped like a wide crescent with neither cabin nor tail. The crafts were flying with a strange wavelike motion. At times they dipped from side to side, and the sun reflected off their silver-blue surfaces. The formation was moving very fast. Arnold later estimated the speed at around 1,300 miles per hour (2,100 km/h), much faster than any known aircraft at the time.

UFO

FLYING SAUCERS

When he reached home, Arnold contacted a reporter, Bill Bequette, at the *East Oregonian*, his local newspaper. Bequette asked how the craft moved. Arnold said, "They flew like a saucer would if you skipped it across water." In his report, Bequette referred to the craft as flying saucers. The term quickly became popular.

On July 4, 1947, the crew of a United Airlines aircraft reported between five and nine disklike objects flying alongside their plane, then suddenly disappearing. This account was in addition to 16 other reported UFO sightings in the same area and on the same day as Arnold's.

THE ROSWELL

On July 8, 1947, a press release from Roswell Army Air Field said a flying saucer had crashed nearby and the wreckage had been recovered. Then the press office at Roswell claimed they had been mistaken and the story went quiet. What really happened at Roswell?

A few hours after the first press release, the public information officer at Roswell issued another, with a photo (below). It stated that the wreckage was not from a flying saucer, but a weather balloon.

THE STORY IS REVIVED

Thirty years later, UFO researcher Stanton Friedman was put in touch with a former intelligence officer, Jesse Marcel, who had served at Roswell. Marcel claimed he had been sent to the crash site to collect the debris. He said he had never believed the weather balloon story. He described the debris as "nothing made on this earth."

INCIDENT

WITNESS INTERVIEWS

By 1980, Friedman had interviewed 62 people. He came to believe that something strange had happened at Roswell and that the United States Air Force (USAF) had covered it up. The witnesses claimed they had seen a UFO performing maneuvers impossible for any aircraft.

EXAMINING THE EVIDENCE

A different kind of cover-up?
Most of the evidence at Roswell was collected decades after the event. An official USAF report admitted there had been a cover-up, but said this was because the crashed craft was a top-secret Mogul high-altitude balloon used for spying on the Soviets. Despite this, many UFOLOGISTS remain convinced that an alien craft, and its occupants, were recovered at Roswell.

ALIEN BODIES?

In 1989, a mortician named Glenn Dennis claimed that the USAF medical team had called him in July 1947. He said they had asked him detailed questions about how to preserve bodies. A USAF photographer then came forward to say he had seen and photographed four alien bodies at the Roswell base.

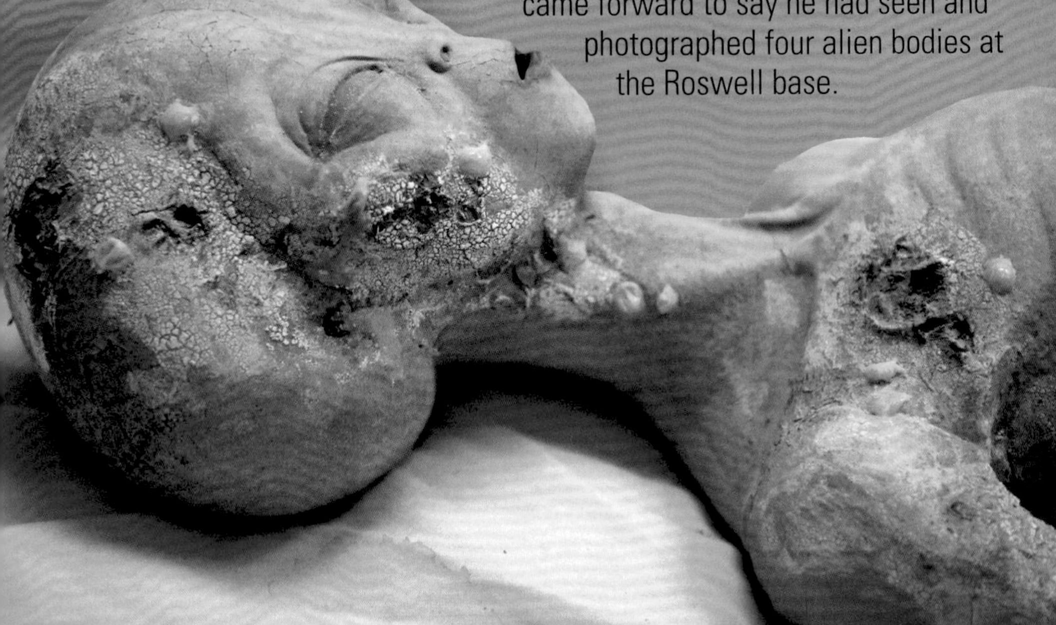

THE MANTELL

On January 7, 1948, a UFO was spotted over Godman Army Airfield in Kentucky. Base commander Colonel Guy Hix SCRAMBLED three P-51 fighter aircraft, which set off in pursuit of the mysterious object.

So what did Mantell and his fellow pilots chase that day? No one knows, but the pilot's death meant that aliens, previously regarded by the public as figures of fun, were suddenly seen as potentially hostile and regarded with deadly seriousness.

GIVING CHASE

As the three aircraft emerged from the clouds, Captain Thomas Mantell (far right) saw the UFO first and gave chase. The other two pilots radioed air traffic control to say they could see the object with Mantell's aircraft behind it. Then the clouds closed in again. The two planes returned to base, but Mantell's aircraft was still climbing in hot pursuit. He sent three radio messages with updates on his progress. Then, there was silence.

INCIDENT

FATAL CRASH

After several minutes of radio silence from Mantell, Hix began to worry. More aircraft were scrambled to search the skies for the mysterious object and for Mantell's P-51, but they found nothing. A few hours later, the wreckage of Mantell's aircraft was found strewn over a large area of countryside. It had obviously broken up at high altitude and fallen to the ground in thousands of pieces.

EYEWITNESS TO MYSTERY

Mantell's final radio messages

"The object is directly ahead of and above me now, moving at about half my speed . . . It looks metallic and it's tremendous in size." A few minutes later: "I'm still climbing . . . I'm trying to close in for a better look." Last message: "It is still above me, making my speed or better. I'm going up to 20,000 feet (6,000 m). If I'm no closer then, I'll abandon the chase."

THE BOTTA

Dr. Enrique Botta was an engineer working on a building project in the rural area of Bahia Blanca in Venezuela. One evening in 1950, he was driving back to his hotel when he saw a strange object resting in a field. He stopped his car to take a look.

INVESTIGATING THE OBJECT

According to Botta, the object was shaped like a domed disk made of silvery metal, but with a surface of jellylike softness. At the side, a door stood open. Passing through this, Botta entered a room where he found three humanoid figures facing a control panel filled with lights. Each was about 4 feet (1.2 m) tall, with a large, bald head. The aliens had their backs to him. When Botta reached out and touched one, he found it was rigid. Thinking the aliens were dead, Botta fled back to his car.

ENCOUNTER

RETURN TO THE SITE

At the hotel, Botta told two colleagues of his discovery. Next morning, the three men returned to the site. The craft had gone and all that remained was a pile of ashes. One of the men touched the pile and his hand turned purple. Then Botta saw a cigar-shaped UFO circling overhead. After a few minutes, it flew off. Later that day, Botta collapsed with a fever and was rushed to a hospital where he was diagnosed with severe sunburn.

FACT HUNTER

Close encounters

Encounters with UFOs are divided into three kinds:

- Close encounters of the first kind (CE1s)—sightings of UFOs
- Close encounters of the second kind (CE2s)—sightings of UFOs and their physical effects, such as crop circles
- Close encounters of the third kind (CE3s)—sightings of aliens

The first reported CE3 took place in 1952. Radio worker William Squyres claimed to have seen an alien at the controls of a disk-shaped UFO hovering above a field in Kansas.

THE SUTTON

On August 21, 1955, Bill Taylor was visiting his neighbor Elmer Sutton at his remote farm in Kentucky. At around 7 P.M., Taylor was fetching water from the well when he saw a disk-shaped UFO floating down behind a line of trees.

The Sutton Encounter marked the start of a series of "little green men" sightings. In separate incidents, several witnesses claimed to have been terrorized by creatures similar to gremlins or goblins. Steven Spielberg's movie *Close Encounters of the Third Kind* was directly inspired by these events.

STRANGE VISITORS

An hour later, Taylor and Sutton saw a strange figure outside the kitchen window. It was 3 feet (1 m) tall, had long apelike arms, and walked upright on short legs. It had a large head, pointed ears, bulging eyes, a slitlike mouth, and emitted a soft, silvery glow. The creature was then joined by several others. Taylor and Sutton picked up their guns and stepped outside. Sutton shouted a challenge. What did these creatures want? One of them ran toward him with its arms raised. Sutton opened fire, knocking the alien onto its back. But after a moment, it stood up and ran off, seemingly unhurt.

ENCOUNTER

UNDER SIEGE

When Taylor and Sutton ran indoors, they heard footsteps on the roof. When Taylor went to investigate, one of the aliens grabbed hold of his hair. Taylor shot the alien. It flipped backward over the roof, then fled into the darkness. For the next three hours, the men took potshots at the aliens whenever they appeared. In the morning, they drove to the local police station and reported their story. The police found evidence of a battle but no aliens.

EYEWITNESS TO MYSTERY

"Something frightened these people"

Elmer Sutton was known locally as a tough guy, not given to flights of fancy. Although his story seemed outlandish, the police were inclined to take it seriously. Police chief Russell Greenwell later commented: "Something frightened these people. Something beyond their comprehension." Despite suffering ridicule, Sutton and Taylor never changed their story. They remained convinced they had been attacked that night and were lucky to have escaped with their lives.

THE SOCORRO

On April 24, 1964, around 5:45 P.M., policeman Lonnie Zamora was driving south from Socorro, New Mexico, in pursuit of a speeding motorist. He suddenly noticed a bluish orange flash in the sky to the west, followed by a roaring explosion. Fearing a nearby dynamite shack had exploded, he gave up his chase and went to investigate.

◄ TWO FIGURES

As Zamora drove down a shallow gully, the flame appeared again. It was cone-shaped. At the top of the gully, Zamora saw an object with two figures standing beside it. The object was oval, whitish silver, and stood on four legs. The figures wore white overalls and may have had rounded caps or helmets.

▸ ZAMORA INVESTIGATES

When Zamora (pictured right) looked again, the figures had vanished. He stepped out of his car and approached the object. As he drew nearer, a roaring began and a bluish orange flame erupted from the base of the craft. Fearing for his life, Zamora turned and ran. Glancing back, he saw the object hovering on its flame above the ground. Next time he looked, the flame and the roaring had stopped and the object hung eerily motionless. Then it moved off silently toward the southwest before vanishing behind some hills.

EXAMINING THE EVIDENCE

Analyzing the traces

When ufologist Dr. Josef Hynek arrived at the site two days later, he found burn marks on the ground where the craft had stood. There were four deep rectangular indentations in the dry soil. These were positioned on the circumference of a circle, and could well have been made by four struts supporting an oval object. Zamora was an excellent witness, highly respected by his colleagues. Hynek concluded that a real, physical event of an unexplained nature had taken place.

INCIDENT AT

Maurice Masse was a farmer in Valensole, France. He had no interest in UFOs and had never seen a futuristic movie or read a science-fiction book. He had no obvious reason to invent a story. Yet what he claimed happened to him one July morning in 1965 sounds like pure fantasy.

WHISTLING SOUND

During a break from his work, Masse heard a whistling sound coming from behind a small hill. When he went to investigate, he found an egg-shaped silver object mounted on six thin, metal legs. Next to it appeared to be two young boys. They were leaning over with their backs to him, pulling at a lavender plant. Thinking they were vandals, Masse crept toward them.

VALENSOLE

PARALYZED

One of the "boys" turned around and whipped out a small gun-shaped object, which he pointed at Masse. The farmer realized suddenly he had been paralyzed. The visitors were about 4 feet (1.2 m) tall with slender bodies, and oval heads with pointy chins, large, slanting eyes, and thin, lipless mouths.

STRANGE STORIES

Similarities with Socorro

Some years after the incident at Valensole, a French UFO investigator sent Masse a drawing of the UFO that had landed at Socorro, New Mexico (see pages 42–43). Masse's reaction was immediate and emphatic: "That is what I saw," he replied. "You see, I was not dreaming and I was not mad."

DEPARTURE

The aliens made strange noises, but their mouths did not move. They floated up through a hatch in the side of their craft, which rose vertically to around 60 feet (18 m), then flew off.

THE EXETER

On September 3, 1965, at 1 A.M, Patrolman Eugene Bertrand was driving along Route 108 near Exeter, New Hampshire, when he saw a car parked at the side of the road. He pulled over and found a woman in some distress. She said her car had been followed by a bright white light in the sky that had hovered over the vehicle before flying off.

◄ MUSCARELLO'S STORY

Bertrand returned to the Exeter police station at 2:30 A.M. There he found Norman Muscarello (pictured left), who was shaking with fear. Muscarello had been walking to Exeter along Route 150 when he saw a group of five red lights swoop down from the sky and hover over a house. The lights began to PULSATE, then suddenly darted toward him. Muscarello dived into a ditch. When he looked again, he saw the lights drop behind a line of trees, as if landing in a field beyond

INCIDENT

SPOOKY LIGHTS

Bertrand drove Muscarello back to the scene of the sighting. Upon leaving the car, the two men suddenly saw a group of red lights rising up behind the trees. As the lights came closer, Bertrand drew his pistol but did not fire. Hiding behind the car, the men watched as the lights approached to within 100 feet (30 m). Bertrand radioed for backup. By the time patrolman David Hunt arrived, the lights had retreated to about 1/3 mile (1/2 km) away.

EXAMINING THE EVIDENCE

Sticking to their story

Bertrand and Hunt made a formal report about the Exeter incident. The Pentagon claimed the men must have witnessed a flight of B-47 military aircraft that had passed over the area. But Bertrand and Hunt pointed out that they had spent many nights driving the highways and were familiar with B-47s. Also, the B-47 flight had passed over around 1:30 A.M. and the sighting had continued until past 3 A.M. Later, the Pentagon reclassified the sighting as unidentified. The Exeter incident is interesting because of the number of witnesses and the fact that the police witnesses went to such lengths to defend their story.

MEN IN

One UFO witness, David Stephens, began to meet regularly with a medical doctor and HYPNOTIST, Herbert Hopkins, to discuss his experience. On September 11, 1976, Hopkins was phoned by a man claiming to be vice president of the New Jersey UFO Research Organization. The man asked if he could pay Hopkins a visit.

STRANGE VISITOR

According to Hopkins, the moment he put the phone down, the man arrived at his home. He was wearing a black suit with sharply creased pants, a black hat, black shoes, a black tie, and gray gloves. Hopkins invited him in.

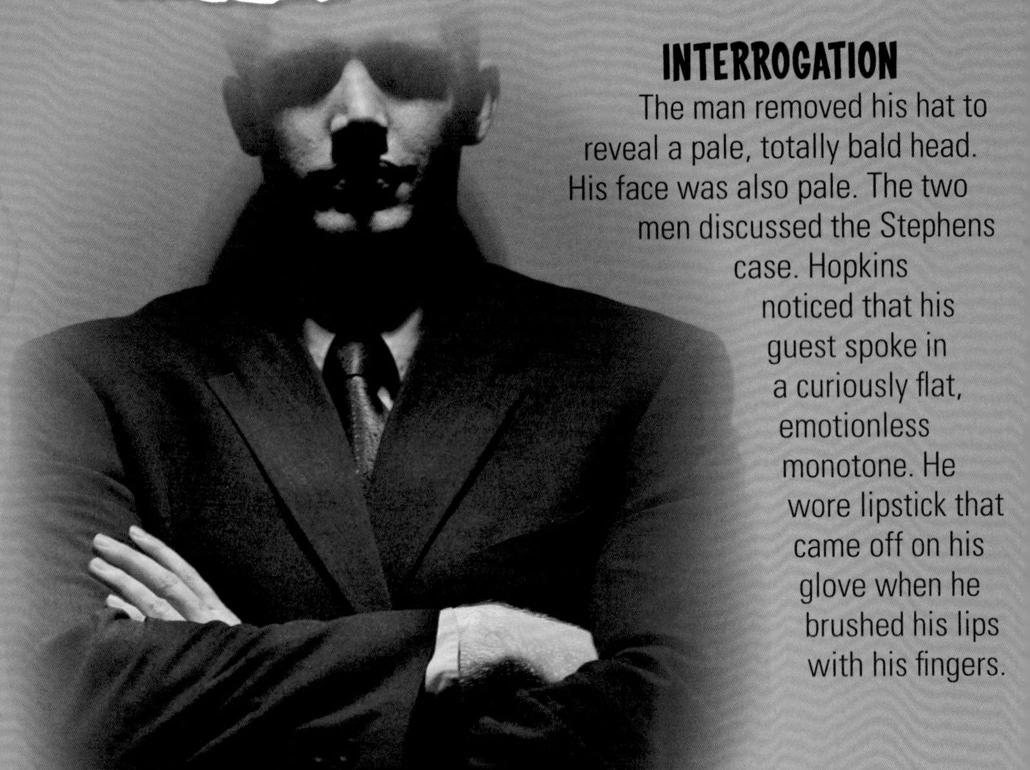

INTERROGATION

The man removed his hat to reveal a pale, totally bald head. His face was also pale. The two men discussed the Stephens case. Hopkins noticed that his guest spoke in a curiously flat, emotionless monotone. He wore lipstick that came off on his glove when he brushed his lips with his fingers.

BLACK

DISAPPEARING TRICK

Suddenly the man asked for a coin. Hopkins handed one over and was surprised to see it vanish from the man's open palm. The man then said he could make a heart vanish from inside a human body just as easily. He told Hopkins to stop working with Stephens and to destroy all his files. Terrified, Hopkins agreed to do so. He later discovered that the New Jersey UFO Research Organization did not exist.

FACT HUNTER

Men in Black

"Men in Black" wear black suits and claim to be officials of secret organizations or government agents. They threaten UFO witnesses to keep quiet about what they have seen. They usually have detailed information on the people they contact. They are often confused by everyday items such as pens or eating utensils. Some ufologists believe Men in Black are aliens or ANDROIDS sent out to maintain the secrecy of alien activity on Earth. Others think they are government agents seeking to hush up UFO sightings. A third theory suggests they are hallucinations caused by the trauma of encountering a UFO.

ENCOUNTER AT

On the evening of October 21, 1978, 20-year-old pilot Frederick Valentich was flying from Melbourne, Australia, to King Island. He took off at 6:19 P.M. and by 7 P.M. was flying over Bass Strait, the stretch of sea between mainland Australia and Tasmania.

NEAR MISS

At 7:06 P.M., Valentich radioed Melbourne Flight Control to ask if there were any other aircraft in the area. Melbourne replied that no known aircraft were around. There was a slight pause, then Valentich reported that a large aircraft showing four bright lights had just flown past 1,000 feet (300 m) above him.

"IT'S NOT AN AIRCRAFT"

At 7:09 P.M., Valentich reported, "It seems to be playing some sort of game with me." Melbourne asked if he could identify the aircraft. "It's not an aircraft," came the surprising response, then, "It's coming for me right now!" Shortly afterward, Valentich seemed to calm down. "I'm orbiting and the thing is orbiting on top of me. It has a green light and a sort of metallic light on the outside."

BASS STRAIT

VANISHED

At 7:12 P.M., Valentich came back on the radio. He said, "Engine is rough and coughing . . . Unknown aircraft is on top of me." There was a burst of static, then silence. Melbourne tried contacting Valentich repeatedly but to no avail. At 7:28 P.M., Melbourne ordered a search to begin. No sign of Valentich or his aircraft was ever found.

EXAMINING THE EVIDENCE

Flying upside down?

Following Valentich's disappearance, there were many attempts to explain what had happened. One theory was that he had somehow turned his aircraft upside down and was seeing the reflection of his own lights in the sea. But Valentich had the UFO in sight for about 7 minutes. If his aircraft had flown upside down for more than 30 seconds, the fuel system would have collapsed.

THE LIVINGSTON

At 10 A.M. on November 9, 1979, forestry worker Robert Taylor was inspecting woodland outside Livingston, Scotland. In a clearing in the forest, he encountered a dark gray, hovering object about 20 feet (6 m) across. It was spherical, with a thin rim around the base.

BLACK SPHERES

Almost at once Taylor saw two black balls with metal spikes drop from beneath the object. Each ball was around 3 feet (1 m) in diameter and rolled toward him on spikes, which made a soft sucking noise as they touched the ground. Before Taylor could retreat, the spheres attached themselves to the legs of his pants. At this point, there was a hissing noise and a burning stench so intense he could barely breathe. The balls began dragging Taylor back toward the gray object. He felt himself grow dizzy and lose consciousness.

When Taylor reached home at 11:30 A.M., his wife assumed he had been attacked. Taylor complained of a headache and kept saying he had been "gassed."

INJURED

Twenty minutes later, when Taylor woke up, facedown on the grass, the strange objects had vanished. His pants were torn, one of his legs was badly bruised, and his chin was cut and bleeding. He couldn't stand up and had to crawl back to his truck. When he got home, he called his boss and told him his story.

EXAMINING THE EVIDENCE

Marks in the soil

The police went to the clearing and examined marks in the soil. They found two parallel tracks, each 8 feet (2.5 m) long and 1 foot (30 cm) wide. There were two circles of holes around these tracks. Each hole was circular and about 4 inches (10 cm) wide and 6 inches (15 cm) deep. There were 40 holes in total, driven into the ground at an angle away from the tracks. No heavy machinery had been used in the clearing for months. The police found the marks to be consistent with Taylor's story.

CHAPTER 3

STRANGE AND

The world is full of strange mysteries, including crop circles, oceans that swallow up ships and aircraft, curious lines in the desert, and legendary lost cities. To date, no one has found a satisfactory explanation for any of them.

MYSTERIOUS FORCES

Crop circles have been appearing in fields for more than 300 years. Some people claim to have seen them being made. They describe an invisible line snaking at high speed through a field, pushing the crops aside. When the line reaches a certain point, it begins to spin around, like the hands on a clock, and presses the crops down flat. When it has completed the circle, the force seems to depart, leaving the crops neatly matted. UFOs have been said to appear over fields the night before the formation of new circles.

STRANGE STORIES

The Mowing-Devil

The Mowing-Devil is the title of an English pamphlet published in 1678. Some people believe it contains the first recorded example of a crop circle. The pamphlet tells of a farmer who was outraged by the sum of money requested by a laborer for mowing his field. The farmer exclaimed he would sooner the Devil mowed it. That night, the field burst into flames, and the following morning it was neatly mowed. The pamphlet's illustration shows a crop circle.

STRANGER

STRANGE EFFECTS?

Curious experiences have been reported near crop circles. Electrical devices have been said to malfunction. Some people have described improved physical well-being; others have reported feelings of nausea, migraines, and fatigue. Animals have been described behaving strangely, with horses and cats becoming nervous, and flocks of birds veering around the circles.

THE BERMUDA

The Bermuda, or Devil's, Triangle is an area of ocean off the southeastern tip of the United States where countless boats and planes have been inexplicably lost. There have certainly been some high-profile disappearances in the region.

In 1918, the USS *Cyclops* vanished in the Bermuda Triangle. The disappearance of the 309-man crew was the single largest loss in U.S. Navy history not related to combat.

MYSTERY OF FLIGHT 19

On December 5, 1945, a squadron of five U.S. Navy Avenger torpedo bombers, known as Flight 19, set off from Florida for the island of Bimini. About 90 minutes into the flight, radio operators received a signal from the commander, Lt. Charles Taylor, saying his compasses weren't working. Then radio contact stalled and search craft were dispatched. One of the rescue planes lost communication and another exploded after take-off. Despite all efforts, Flight 19 had vanished.

TRIANGLE

WILD IDEAS

There are various theories about the loss of Flight 19 and other transportation in the area. Some blame the mystery on visiting UFOs near Bermuda, or on evil marine creatures. Others say the Triangle is a gateway to another dimension. Further theories blame huge clouds of methane gas escaping from the seabed.

NATURAL EXPLANATIONS

The U.S. Coast Guard maintains that losses in the area have been caused by bad weather and human error. They say the Bermuda Triangle is no more treacherous than any other waterway.

STRANGE STORIES

The Dragon's Triangle

Off the west coast of Japan lies the Dragon's Triangle. Japanese sailors call it *Ma no Umi*, meaning "Sea of the Devil." Some say they've seen red lights and heard terrible noises. Others say the legendary sea monster *Li-Lung* lives there. In 1952, after numerous losses, the Japanese government dispatched a research vessel, the *Kiao Maru* No.5, to study the area. It disappeared without a trace.

THE NAZCA

Ancient, enormous, mysterious markings are etched across the Nazca Desert in Peru. Many of them are of people, animals, and plants. But there are also hundreds of randomly spaced lines, some crisscrossing, others in the shape of triangles and squares. Who made these lines and what are they for?

It is believed that the lines were created by the sophisticated Nazca people more than 1,600 years ago, using gravel and soil. One line is over 8.7 miles (14 km) long.

AERIAL VIEW

Local people have always known about the lines, which appear to be centuries old. However, when regular air travel began in South America in the 1930s, a truly remarkable feature of the lines was revealed. They made up pictures and designs, but these were so huge that they could only be appreciated from the air!

LINES

WHAT WERE THEY FOR?

Many theories seek to explain the Nazca Lines. Some say they were a special site for religious ceremonies, or an indication of underground sources of water. One theory even suggests that the Nazca people were early aviators who developed the world's first hot-air balloon. Another suggests the lines were runways for alien visitors!

EYEWITNESS TO MYSTERY

Cleansing wind

Dr. Maria Reiche explains why the lines have lasted for so long: "There are extremely strong winds here, even sandstorms, but the sand never deposits over the drawings. On the contrary, the wind has a cleansing effect, taking away all the loose material. This way, the drawings were preserved for thousands of years. It is also one of the driest places on Earth, drier than the Sahara. It rains only half an hour every two years!"

THE PIRI REIS

In 1929, a map was unearthed in Istanbul, Turkey. Drawn on gazelle skin, it shows the Atlantic, the Americas, and Antarctica. But the remarkable thing about this map is that it challenges our understanding of exploration history.

The Piri Reis map is named after Muhiddin Piri, an admiral in the Ottoman-Turkish navy. He created the map in 1513, using his knowledge from traveling the world.

MYSTERIOUS MAPPING

The Piri Reis map was made just 21 years after Columbus landed in the Americas—three centuries before Antarctica was discovered. Many believe that this map shows the coastline of Antarctica under the ice. But Antarctic ice is up to 2.5 miles (4 km) thick and the land under it wasn't mapped until 1949. The map also places the Falkland Islands at the correct latitude, even though they weren't discovered until 1592. Greenland is shown as three separate islands. This is strange as it wasn't until the 1950s that scientists discovered this to be true.

MAP

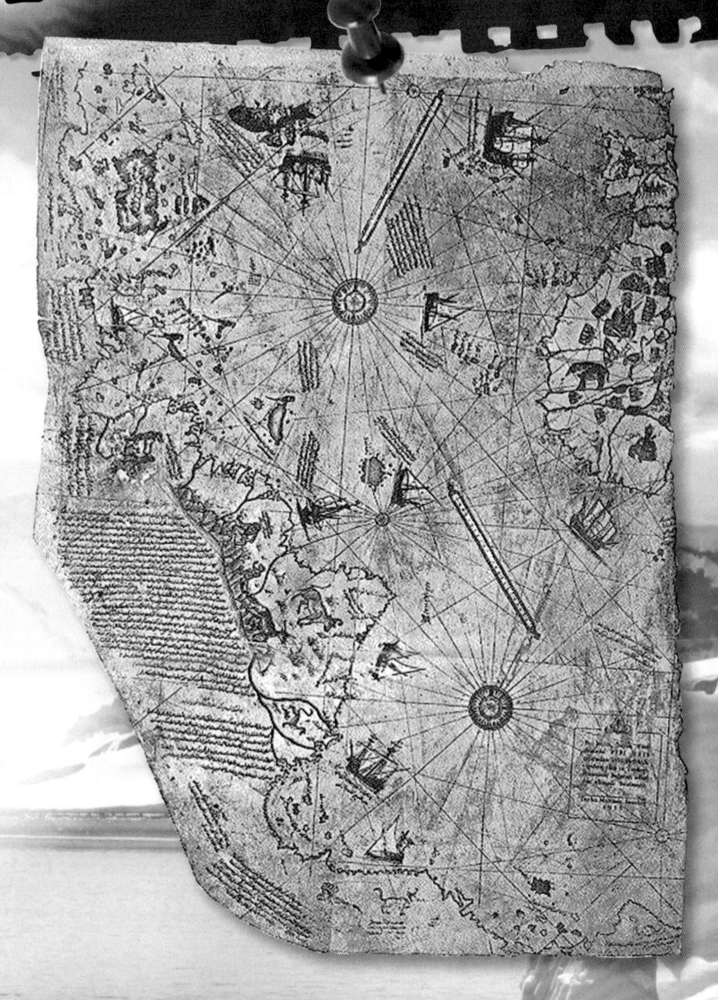

ALIEN CHART?

Some people believe that an ancient race of humans, using advanced but now lost technology, recorded the details of Antarctica before it was covered with ice. Others suggest that alien creatures mapped the planet and left their charts behind for humankind.

EXAMINING THE EVIDENCE

Antarctica—an inspired guess?

Experts say that many maps from this time include imaginary continents in the South Atlantic. Piri might just have been lucky with his guesswork. They say Antarctica has been ice-covered for hundreds of thousands of years. But others claim the continent may have been ice-free as recently as 6,000 years ago.

EASTER

Easter Island lies some 2,286 miles (3,680 km) off the coast of Peru in the South Pacific. Unknown to the world, it was discovered on Easter Sunday, 1722, by Jakob Roggeveen, a Dutch admiral. Roggeveen was astonished to find enormous carved stone figures on the island. Who had put them there? What was their purpose?

THE MOAI

The INDIGENOUS people of Easter Island call this volcanic land Rapa Nui. They had lived there for more than 1,000 years, cut off from the rest of the world. Over time, they had erected more than 1,000 huge statues, or *moai*. Many of the statues stood on stone platforms called *ahus.*

ISLAND

STRANGE STORIES

Statue toppling

After Roggeveen's visit in 1722, the moai were gradually toppled. The last one fell in 1868. This was possibly the result of conflict among the islanders. The moai were usually toppled forward, so their faces were hidden and, often, their necks were broken. Today, around 50 moai have been re-erected on their platforms or in museums.

WHO, WHEN, HOW, AND WHY?

Some believe the islanders were descended from a Polynesian tribe, while others believe they came from South America. They probably settled on the island in about AD 500 and began building the statues soon afterward. Experts believe the statues were built out of stone from the walls of volcanic craters. But how these enormous statues were made without modern tools, then transported and moved into position on the stone platforms still remains a mystery.

THE GREAT

The Ancient Egyptians built the pyramids to show the importance of their dead kings and aid their passage to the afterlife. But the largest of them all, the Great Pyramid of Khufu at Giza, is shrouded in mystery.

King Khufu was a ruthless ruler, obsessed with wealth and founding a dynasty. To this end, he built several pyramids and fathered 24 children!

STRANGE SHAFTS

The Great Pyramid was built around 2500 BC at Giza, near Cairo. It contains a great number of chambers and corridors, including mysterious shafts extending from what are known as the king's and queen's chambers. Some experts think they were designed to allow Khufu's soul to travel to the stars in the afterlife.

PYRAMID

EMPTY INTERIOR

It is assumed that the Great Pyramid was the tomb of Khufu and a storehouse for his treasures. But when the pyramid was opened in AD 820, nothing was found but an empty stone SARCOPHAGUS (an elaborate coffin).

OTHER THEORIES

Without hard evidence to prove that the Great Pyramid was a burial place, other theories have sprung up. Some say it is a record of all events past, present, and future. The passageways are timelines and the intersections are great happenings. Some mathematicians claim the Great Pyramid demonstrates knowledge of the true value of the mathematical number PI. Other people claim it was built by aliens as a landing beacon for their next trip to Earth.

STONEHENGE

This world-famous circle of standing stones on Salisbury Plain in Wiltshire, England, was built between 3000 BC and 1900 BC. How did ancient people build such a vast structure, and what were their reasons for doing so?

Every year, people still gather at Stonehenge on the SUMMER SOLSTICE, the longest day of the year. They celebrate as they watch the sun rise over the stones.

BUILT BY GIANTS?

The building of Stonehenge involved transporting and erecting huge blocks of stone. Some stories tell that giants brought the stones from Africa to Ireland. The stones were then moved to England during the reign of King Arthur. Archaeological evidence suggests that Stonehenge was built between 3,000 and 5,000 years ago and that the stones came from South Wales. But how the stones were brought to the site still remains a mystery.

WHAT WAS IT USED FOR?

Stonehenge may have been used as a burial site, as shallow holes in the area have been found to contain cremated bones. It may also have been an observatory or giant lunar calendar. In 1965, the astronomer Gerald S. Hawkins claimed that Stonehenge was a prehistoric computer, designed by ancient Britons to predict ECLIPSES.

STRANGE STORIES

Stone circle at Castlerigg

Castlerigg Stone Circle in the Lake District is one of the oldest stone circles in Britain. It was built around 3000 BC and is made up of 38 stones of various heights positioned in a ring. Unique among stone circles in Britain, it has a rectangular arrangement of stones inside the ring. There is also a slight mound in the center. Is this a burial chamber?

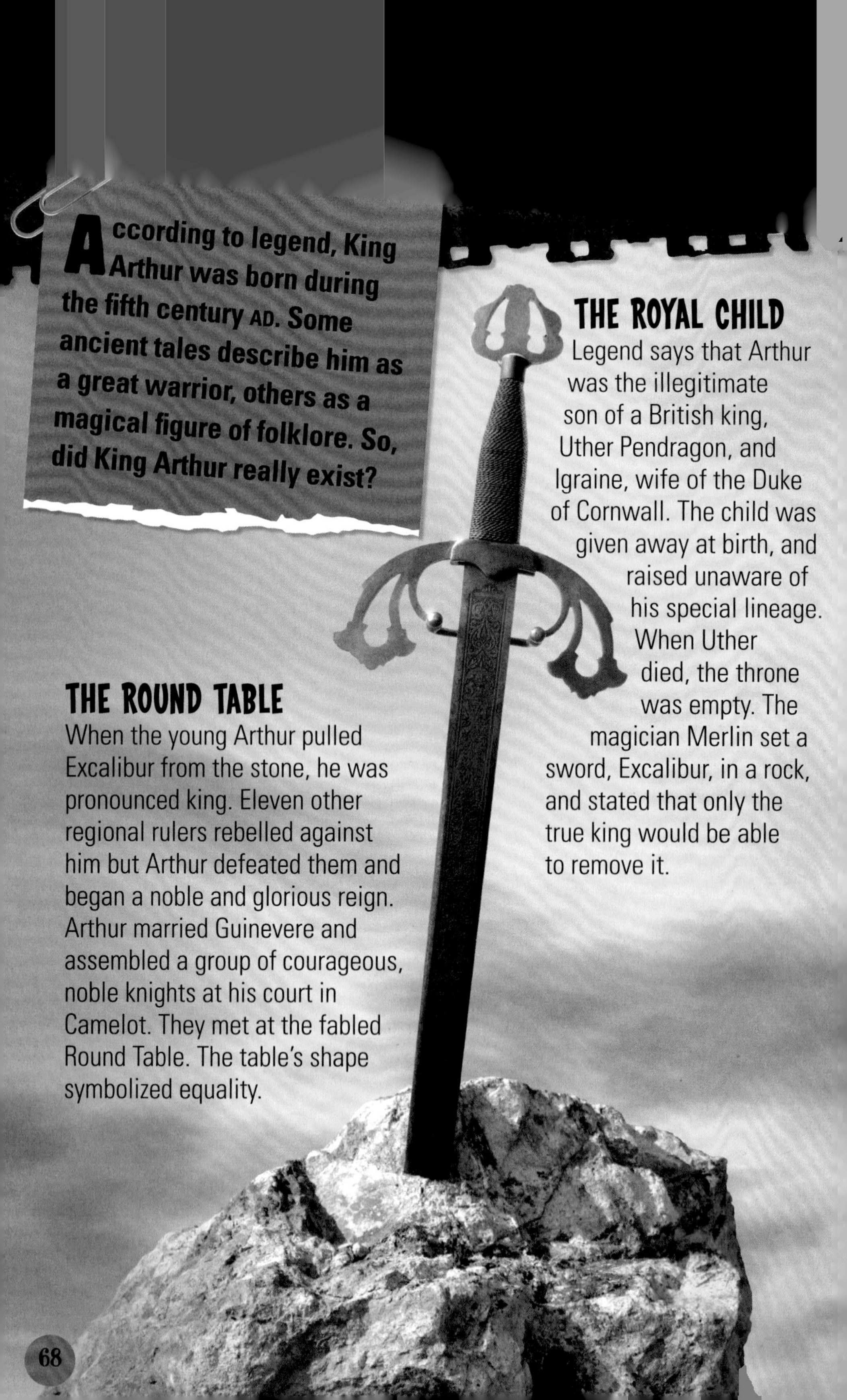

According to legend, King Arthur was born during the fifth century AD. Some ancient tales describe him as a great warrior, others as a magical figure of folklore. So, did King Arthur really exist?

THE ROYAL CHILD

Legend says that Arthur was the illegitimate son of a British king, Uther Pendragon, and Igraine, wife of the Duke of Cornwall. The child was given away at birth, and raised unaware of his special lineage. When Uther died, the throne was empty. The magician Merlin set a sword, Excalibur, in a rock, and stated that only the true king would be able to remove it.

THE ROUND TABLE

When the young Arthur pulled Excalibur from the stone, he was pronounced king. Eleven other regional rulers rebelled against him but Arthur defeated them and began a noble and glorious reign. Arthur married Guinevere and assembled a group of courageous, noble knights at his court in Camelot. They met at the fabled Round Table. The table's shape symbolized equality.

MERLIN

In many stories, the wizard Merlin is shown acting as advisor to King Arthur. Merlin's gifts of prophecy and magical power were used by Arthur to help control rebellions and counter the black magic of sorceress Morgan le Fey.

EXAMINING THE EVIDENCE

Legendary leader

Historical evidence for an Arthur figure can be found in a sixth-century work by Gildas, which refers to Ambrosius Aurelianus, a leader of British soldiers. A seventh-century manuscript called *Vita Sancti Columbae* states that Arthur was the son of King Aidan. This document also describes Arthur's last battle against the Picts, a Scottish tribe.

GHOST

On November 7, 1872, the ship *Mary Celeste* left New York bound for Italy with a cargo of alcohol. On board were the captain, his family, and a crew of seven. On December 5, in the mid-Atlantic, the crew of another ship, the *Dei Gratia*, spotted the *Mary Celeste* sailing out of control ahead of them.

DESERTED

The captain of the *Dei Gratia* sent a group to investigate the *Mary Celeste*. They found the ship deserted, but in seaworthy condition and well-stocked with food and water. Only the navigation equipment and lifeboat were missing.

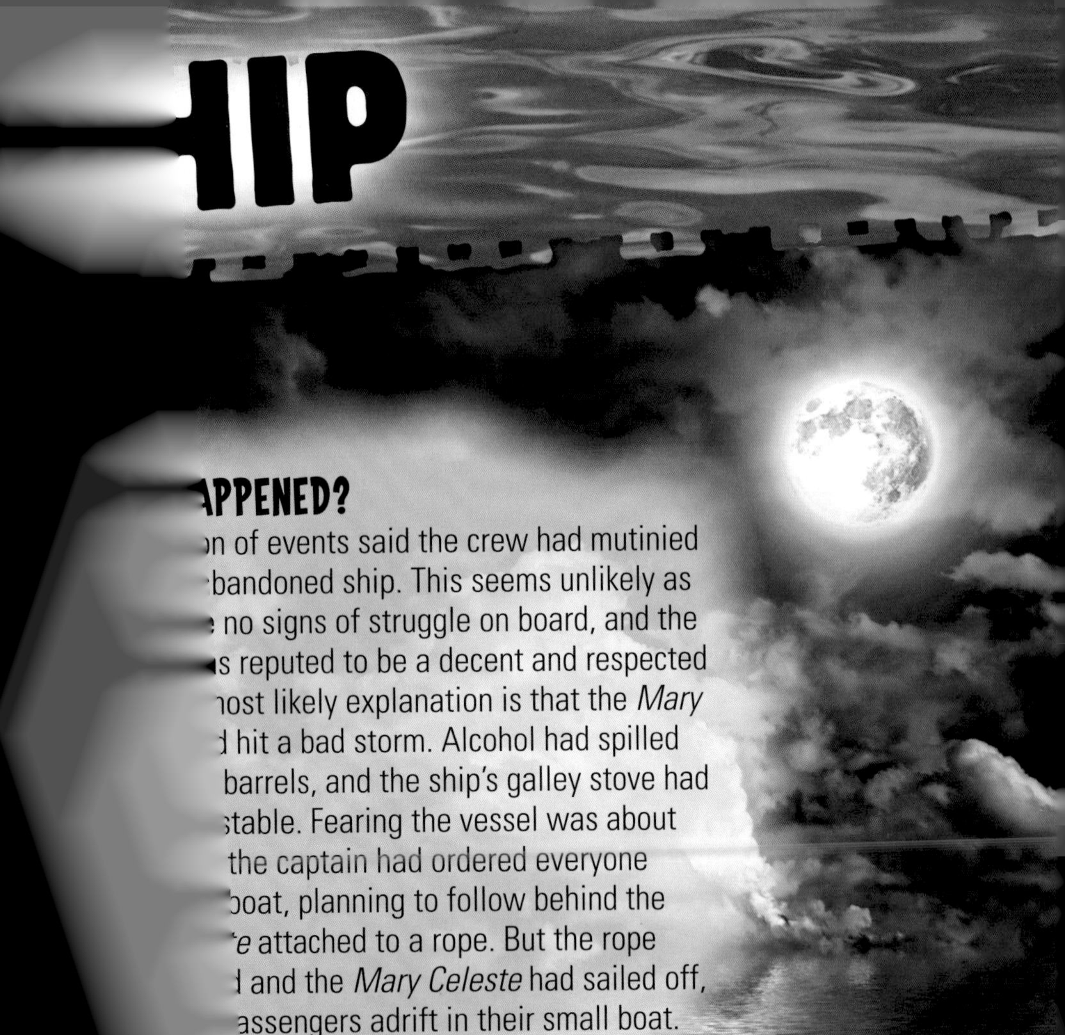

APPENED?

on of events said the crew had mutinied
bandoned ship. This seems unlikely as
no signs of struggle on board, and the
s reputed to be a decent and respected
most likely explanation is that the *Mary*
d hit a bad storm. Alcohol had spilled
barrels, and the ship's galley stove had
stable. Fearing the vessel was about
the captain had ordered everyone
boat, planning to follow behind the
e attached to a rope. But the rope
d and the *Mary Celeste* had sailed off,
assengers adrift in their small boat.

FACT HUNTER

Ghost ships

Ghost ships are vessels found adrift with the entire crew either missing or dead. The Dutch SCHOONER *Hermania* and the ship *Marathon* were both found abandoned but in perfect working order around the same time as the *Mary Celeste*. The *Mary Celeste* owes its fame mainly to the efforts of the Sherlock Holmes author Sir Arthur Conan Doyle, who wrote a story about it.

CHAPTER 4

LOST

Legend says that Atlantis was a beautiful, rich, and powerful island nation. According to Plato, the ancient Greek philosopher, in 9000 BC, Atlantis sank beneath the ocean in a single day and night. Similarly, the land of Lemuria disappeared without a trace. If these lost worlds really existed, what caused them to vanish so suddenly?

IMPERIAL CITY

According to Plato, the island of Atlantis was mountainous and lushly forested. Below the towering dormant volcano of Mount Atlas was a fertile plain irrigated by a network of canals. South of the plain stood the city of Atlantis, capital of a mighty oceanic empire. The city of Atlantis was composed of CONCENTRIC circles of land and water, connected by bridged canals. Each artificial island was surrounded by high walls and mighty watchtowers.

EXAMINING THE EVIDENCE

Did Atlantis exist?

Atlantologists (seekers of Atlantis) argue that a large landmass may once have existed in the location of the Mid-Atlantic Ridge. This area of ocean floor certainly suffers from earthquakes and volcanoes. However, most Plato scholars believe his account of Atlantis was imaginary. Plato's story may have been inspired by the island of Thera in the Mediterranean Sea, destroyed by a volcanic eruption in about 1600 BC. The island of Santorini, off Greece, is all that remains of Thera.

FORMER GLORY

The city of Atlantis was capital of a mighty empire. Below is an artist's impression of the architecture of Atlantis, with a great temple rising above the rest of the city.

WHAT WAS

Lemuria, or Mu, was an island said to have existed long ago, before sinking inexplicably beneath the ocean. The island's people were called Lemurians. Whether Mu was in the Pacific or the Indian Ocean is a matter for debate.

Some people claim that the Lemurians escaped from their sunken island and moved beneath Mount Shasta in northern California, where they can still occasionally be seen.

PACIFIC CULTURE

While the Atlanteans were said to have been an advanced, warlike people, the Lemurians were simple seafarers. They sailed the world to spread their spiritual beliefs, building ceremonial centers, sacred sculptures, and roads. Mu's influence can apparently be seen in statues such as the moai of Easter Island (pictured right). When Mu was swallowed up by the ocean, the Lemurians fled to Melanesia, Polynesia, and Central and South America.

LEMURIA?

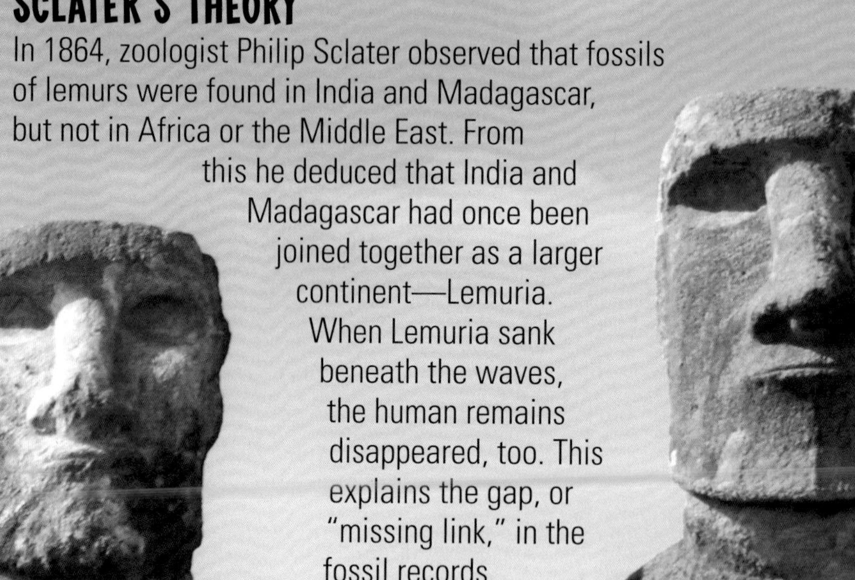

SCLATER'S THEORY

In 1864, zoologist Philip Sclater observed that fossils of lemurs were found in India and Madagascar, but not in Africa or the Middle East. From this he deduced that India and Madagascar had once been joined together as a larger continent—Lemuria. When Lemuria sank beneath the waves, the human remains disappeared, too. This explains the gap, or "missing link," in the fossil records.

THE SEARCH

In 1985, a scuba instructor was diving in the waters off Yonaguni, an island in Japan's Okinawa island chain. The diver found himself confronted by what appeared to be a great stone building. The photographs he took of the structure sparked national interest.

UNDERWATER CITY?

ARCHAEOLOGISTS examined the photographs, but could no structure was natural or human-made. In 1986, another dive waters was shocked to discover a massive underwater arch huge stone blocks. They were beautifully fitted together in t of prehistoric masonry. By the autumn of 1986, five more ap human-made structures had been found near three Japanes The formations seemed to be made up of paved streets and altar-like formations, and grand staircases leading to broad pla. So far, no internal passages or chambers have been found.

LEMURIA

EXPLORING THE RUINS

In 1998, divers found yet another seemingly human-made underwater ruin near the islet of Okinoshima, more than 600 miles (966 km) from Okinawa. It was a row of four stone columns, each 23–33 feet (7–10 m) across and almost 100 feet (30 m) high. One of them featured a spiral staircase winding around its exterior. Below is an artist's impression of the sunken monument lying in the waters off the Japanese island of Yonaguni.

Some people believe that these structures are the remains of Lemuria. They say that either the sea level rose suddenly or the land collapsed, submerging all the buildings.

EXAMINING THE EVIDENCE

Did Lemuria exist?

The scientific community no longer believes that Lemuria existed. According to the theory of PLATE TECTONICS, accepted now by all GEOLOGISTS, Madagascar and India were indeed once part of the same continent. However, plate movement caused the original landmass to break apart very slowly over millions of years. It did not sink beneath the sea.

ISLAND

Frozen COMETS, ASTEROIDS, and undersea volcanoes . . . what exactly were the strange PHENOMENA that destroyed the mighty civilizations of Atlantis and Lemuria?

COMETS AND ASTEROIDS

Atlantologists point to two major comet impacts that could have destroyed Atlantis. The first occurred in about 2200 BC and the second in 1198 BC. This seems to agree with historical records. Plato and the Roman scholar Varo wrote of floods that took place around 2200 BC.

DESTRUCTION

In the year AD 79, Mount Vesuvius erupted and buried the town of Pompeii, Italy, under a layer of lava and ash. The remains of the town and the people who died there were only uncovered more than 1,600 years later.

VOLCANIC ERUPTIONS

Around 1490 BC, a series of geological upheavals appears to have brought great destruction to the Pacific region. At this time, Japan's Mount Sanbe and Alaska's Mount Aniakchak erupted, spewing ash into the atmosphere. The volcanoes of Rabaul in Papua New Guinea and Mauna Kea in Hawaii also exploded. Could the combined effects of these eruptions have been sufficient to destroy Lemuria?

SEEKERS OF

Following the collapse of the ancient civilizations of Greece and Rome, Plato's story of Atlantis was forgotten. However, the story was revived in the seventeenth century by the German Jesuit priest Athanasius Kircher.

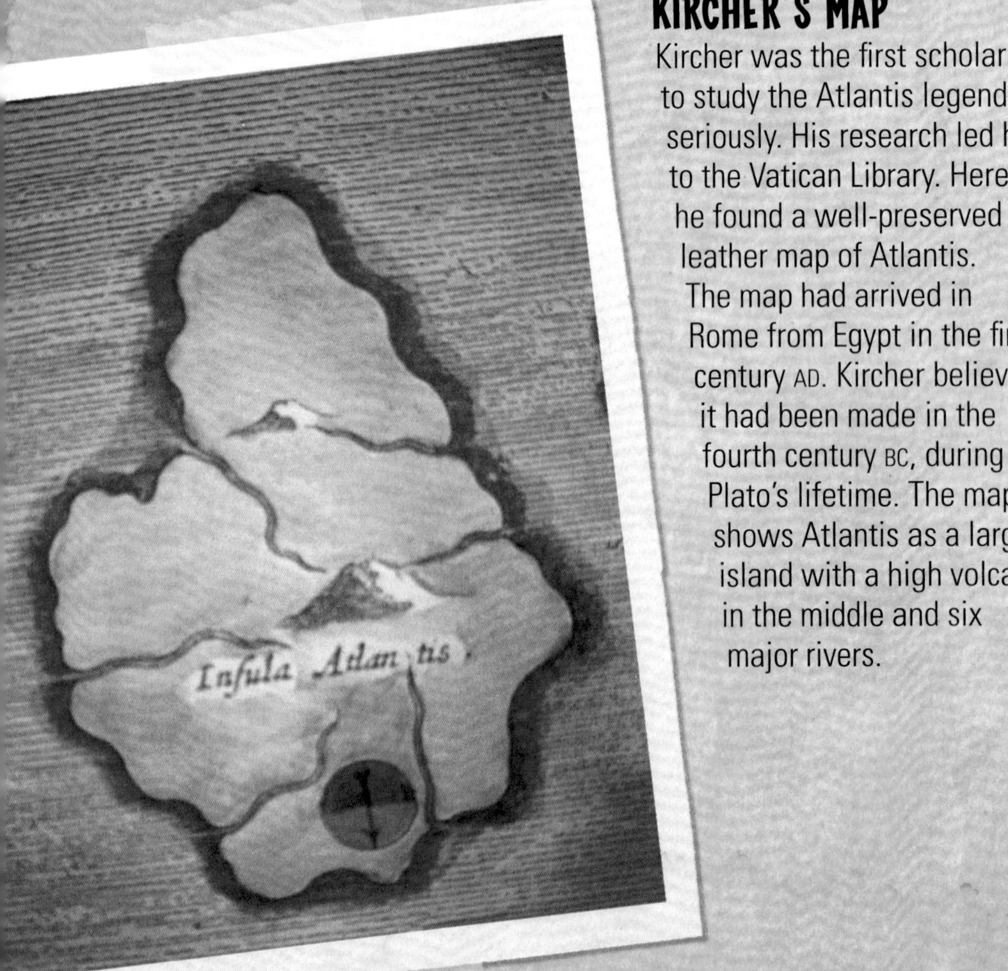

KIRCHER'S MAP

Kircher was the first scholar to study the Atlantis legend seriously. His research led him to the Vatican Library. Here he found a well-preserved leather map of Atlantis. The map had arrived in Rome from Egypt in the first century AD. Kircher believed it had been made in the fourth century BC, during Plato's lifetime. The map shows Atlantis as a large island with a high volcano in the middle and six major rivers.

ATLANTIS

According to Plato, Atlantis was ruled by five sets of male twins, the sons of Poseidon, the Greek God of the sea. The island was named after the oldest son, Atlas, who was the supreme ruler.

RUDBECK

Olaus Rudbeck (1630–1702) was a Swedish professor of medicine and amateur archaeologist who found evidence for Atlantis through excavations and research in his own country. He claimed that Scandinavian myths and archaeological evidence proved that some survivors from Atlantis had come to Sweden. Their influence, he said, had led to the rise of the VIKINGS.

DONNELLY AND BERLITZ

The man who did the most to bring Atlantis to the attention of the wider public was Ignatius Donnelly (1831–1901), a U.S. congressman and founder of Atlantology (pictured). Donnelly's 1882 book, *Atlantis, the Antediluvian World*, was a bestseller and is still published in more than a dozen languages. Later, Charles Berlitz (1914–2003), a talented linguist, concluded that many modern and ancient languages derive from a single prehistoric source, which he traced to Atlantis.

TECHNOLOGY

According to Atlantologists, the lost civilization was incredibly technologically advanced. The people of Atlantis apparently mastered flight thousands of years before the Wright brothers invented the airplane.

ANCIENT AVIATORS?

At the end of the nineteenth century, an ancient wooden artifact resembling a model airplane was excavated near the Nile River in Egypt. Sources found in India refer to floating temples called *vimanas* (shown below). The Incas of Peru told stories of a hero called Kon-Tiki Viracocha who rose high into the air aboard a flying temple. In southwestern North America, the Hopi Indians spoke of *pauwvotas*, airborne vehicles flown over immense distances. Atlantologists believe that these folk memories describe lost technological creations by skilled Atlanteans.

Some people have said the Atlanteans were aliens from another planet who arrived before humankind existed. This explains why they were so advanced.

OF ATLANTIS

BUILDERS

The Atlanteans are believed to have excelled in building. The Great Pyramid is largest of the Egyptian pyramids. From whom did the Egyptians acquire their sophisticated building skills? According to some legends, Thoth, an Atlantean, was the Great Pyramid's chief architect. However, it is believed that Khufu's adviser, Hemiunu, was the original architect. Thoth was an Egyptian god, and was given credit for a lot of things, including the 365-day calendar!

THE SEARCH FOR

In 1949, a curious formation was discovered on the floor of the Atlantic Ocean. It consisted of a large mound surrounded by mountains. Its highest peak was a volcano that had collapsed beneath the sea during the past 12,000 years. Could this be Atlantis?

SAND AND ELEPHANT BONES

Expeditions to the undersea mound have retrieved freshwater sand, algae, and rocks formed on dry land, all of which suggest that it was once an island. Even elephant bones have been dredged from the area, seeming to match Plato's story that these creatures inhabited Atlantis. In 1974, cameras aboard a Soviet research vessel, *Academician Petrovsky*, captured images resembling human-made ruins. Most of these appeared around the peak of Mount Ampere off the coast of Portugal, 213 feet (65 m) below the surface.

ATLANTIS

MYSTERIOUS MOUNDS

The mysterious undersea formations were discovered in 1947 and named the Horseshoe Seamounts. So could these be the submerged remains of Atlantis? The estimated dimensions of the site are similar to those given by Plato. Mount Ampere is also situated in the south, in the same position as Mount Atlas in Plato's description of Atlantis.

FACT HUNTER

The Horseshoe Seamounts

If a ruined city does exist on Mount Ampere, it will be covered with many layers of mud and possibly lava rock. No device has yet been invented that is capable of penetrating such thick layers at this depth. Even if the underwater site really is Atlantis, the disaster that was powerful enough to sink an entire island is unlikely to have left much in the way of artifacts and other cultural evidence.

THE SEARCH

In March 2003, amateur explorers Greg and Lora Little were snorkeling off the island of Andros in the Caribbean when they came across a giant underwater platform made from massive stone blocks.

The Andros platform has six alternating bands of stone. This suggests an Atlantean connection, as Plato wrote that the number six was sacred to the Atlanteans.

THE ANDROS PLATFORM

The platform was 1,502 feet (458 m) long and 164 feet (50 m) wide. Its regular appearance and square-cut blocks suggested it could have been a dock or a port of some kind. In the following years, more discoveries were made at Andros, including a long stone wall 6 miles (10 km) north of the island. Atlantologists believe the remains could have been an outpost of the Atlantean Empire.

Here, a deep-sea submarine dives into the seas around Bimini in the Bahamas in search of evidence of Atlantis.

CONTINUES

BIMINI ROAD

Bimini Road is an underwater rock formation near the island of Bimini in the Bahamas. The structure is made of huge square blocks that run in a J-shaped pattern across the seabed for about 2,600 feet (792 m). The road contains what appear to be several angular KEYSTONES with notches to join them together. This resembles a prehistoric building style seen in the ancient Inca settlements of Cuzco and Machu Picchu in Peru. The wall of Lixus in Morocco in north Africa is also made of huge blocks of square unmortared stone fitted perfectly together. Could these walls be evidence of Atlantean building skill?

BIMINI STONE

Pictured, right, is Atlantis researcher Vanda Osman with a block of stone removed from the Bimini Wall.

LOST WORLDS

Atlantis and Lemuria may be humanity's most famous lost civilizations, but other phantom worlds play a powerful role in the mythology of different peoples. These fabled lands, and the riches they may contain, have tempted many explorers to try to find them.

Hernando Cortés was one of Spain's most successful CONQUISTADORS. Although he never found the mythic "seven cities of gold," he conquered the Aztec Empire.

EL DORADO

When Spanish explorers reached South America in the early 16th century, they heard stories about a tribe of natives high in the Andes mountains in what is now Colombia. When a new ruler rose to power, his rule began with a ceremony at Lake Guatavita. Accounts of the ceremony vary, but they say the new ruler was covered with gold dust, and that gold and precious jewels were thrown into the lake to appease a god that lived underwater. The Spanish believed that the king's city, El Dorado, existed somewhere in Colombia and spent several centuries searching for it. But El Dorado was never found.

OF THE AMERICAS

SEVEN CITIES OF GOLD

In around AD 714, as the North African MOORISH army captured the Spanish city of Mérida, seven Christian bishops and their followers fled across the Atlantic by ship. It was rumored they landed on another continent where they built seven cities rich in gold and precious stones. When the Spanish invaders conquered Mexico in 1519, they searched eagerly for these legendary cities, but never found them.

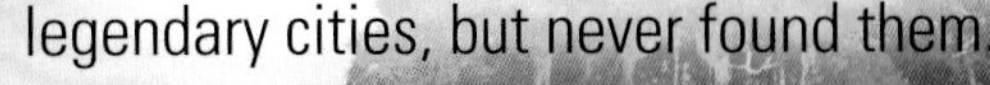

TEOTIHUACÁN

High on a plateau in central Mexico lie the remains of a city that continues to perplex archaeologists and historians. Nobody knows who built it or why it was mysteriously abandoned. At its peak, the city had 200,000 inhabitants. So what happened at Teotihuacán?

MYSTIC CITY

The building of the city began around 200 BC. The major structures were built from the first century AD. The city reached the height of its power and population between the fifth and seventh centuries. But who lived there?

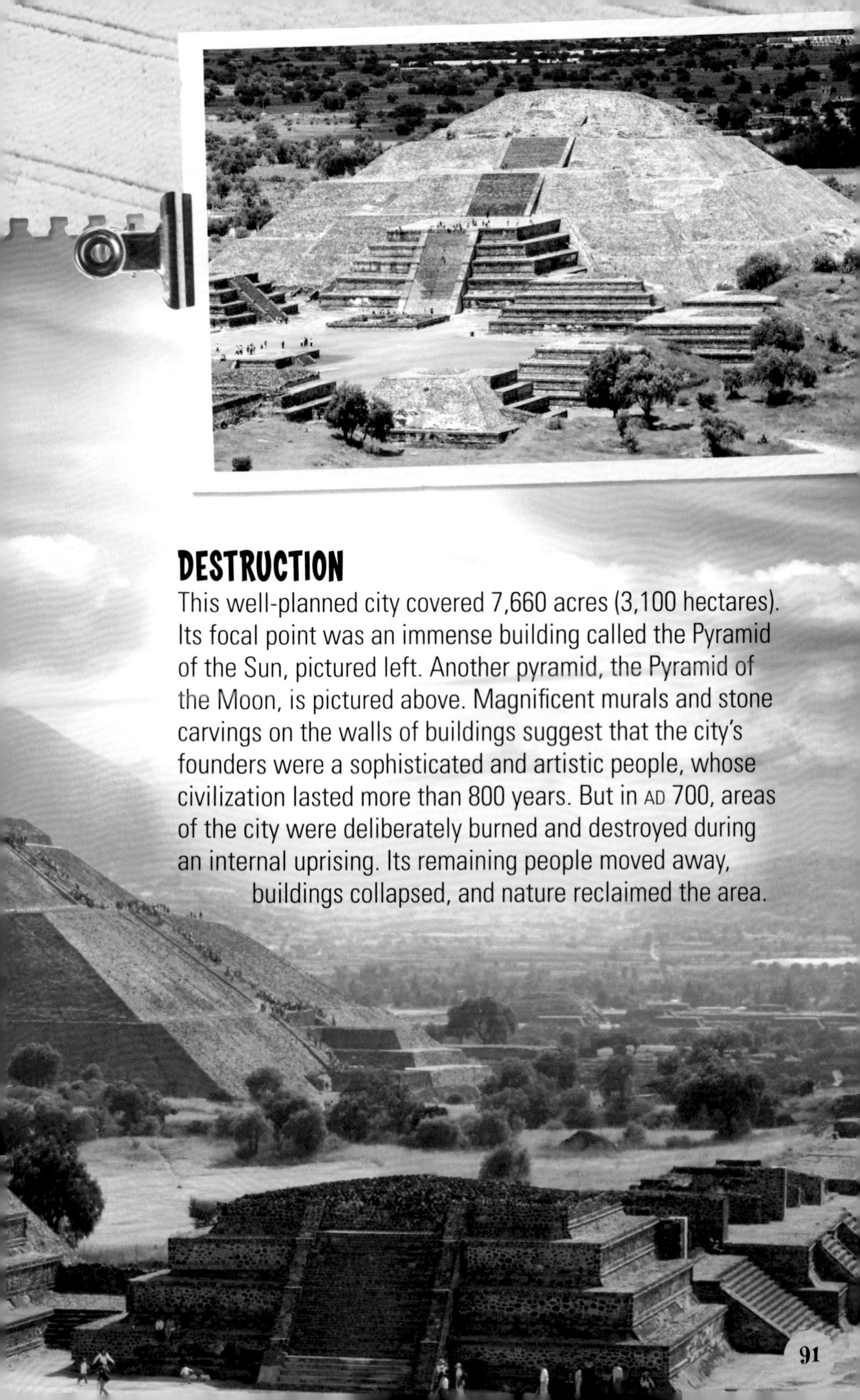

DESTRUCTION

This well-planned city covered 7,660 acres (3,100 hectares). Its focal point was an immense building called the Pyramid of the Sun, pictured left. Another pyramid, the Pyramid of the Moon, is pictured above. Magnificent murals and stone carvings on the walls of buildings suggest that the city's founders were a sophisticated and artistic people, whose civilization lasted more than 800 years. But in AD 700, areas of the city were deliberately burned and destroyed during an internal uprising. Its remaining people moved away, buildings collapsed, and nature reclaimed the area.

LOST WORLDS

From Thule to Hyperborea, how many extinct civilizations lie frozen and hidden away in the world's icy northern regions?

THULE

Thule was a mysterious Arctic realm that was supposedly visited by the ancient Greek explorer Pytheas in the fourth century BC. Pytheas wrote that Thule was a six-day sail north of Britain and was near the "frozen sea." Later, writers placed Thule northwest of Britain and Ireland and beyond the Faroes Islands in the north Atlantic, which means it must have been Iceland. But who were the people Pytheas claimed to have found there? He described them as farming people, producing grain, fruit, dairy products, and honey. Mysteriously, Iceland was not inhabited until the Vikings arrived there in the ninth century AD.

OF THE NORTH

HYPERBOREA

In Greek mythology, Hyperborea, meaning "beyond the north wind," was a mythical land existing far to the north. In this place, the Greeks said, the sun shone for 24 hours a day. Beyond the Arctic Circle, the sun does indeed shine for 24 hours a day for half the year. According to the ancient Greeks, the Hyperboreans were sun worshippers. Some modern researchers have suggested that Hyperborea could in fact have been Britain. The description of the Hyperboreans' great temple is similar to Stonehenge (above).

Hyperborea was viewed by the Greeks as a kind of paradise, where everyone lived to a thousand years of age and all were completely happy. The Greeks also believed Apollo, the sun god, spent his winters there.

GLOSSARY

android (AN-droyd) A robot made to look like a human.

archaeologists (ahr-kee-AH-luh-jist) People who study human history and prehistory by excavating sites and analyzing physical remains.

asteroid (AS-teh-royd) A small rocky body orbiting the Sun. A few asteroids enter Earth's atmosphere as meteors.

cast (KAST) A three-dimensional shape, such as a footprint, made by shaping a material (such as plaster of Paris) in a mold.

comet (KAH-mit) A celestial object consisting of a nucleus of ice and dust and, when near the sun, a "tail" of gas and dust particles.

concentric (kon-CEN-tryk) Describes circles or other shapes that share the same center, the larger ones surrounding the smaller.

conquistadors (kon-KEES-ta-doors) Leaders in the Spanish conquest of America in the sixteenth century.

cryptid (KRIP-tid) A creature that appears in stories, rumors, and legends, but whose existence is not recognized by science.

cryptozoologist (krip-tuh-zoh-O-luh-jist) A person who studies cryptids.

eclipse (ih-KLIPS) An obscuring of the light from a celestial body by the passage of another body between it and the observer.

geologist (jee-AH-luh-jist) A scientist who studies Earth's physical structure and substance, its history, and the processes that act on it.

hallucination (huh-loo-suh-NAY-shun) An experience involving the apparent perception of something not present.

hoax (HOKES) A plan intended to trick someone into believing something that isn't true.

humanoid (HYOO-muh-noyd) Having an appearance resembling that of a human.

hypnotist (hip-NOH-tist) A practitioner who places another person in a state of consciousness in which he or she appears to lose the power of voluntary action and responds to the hypnotist's directions.

indigenous (inn-DIJ-en-us) Living in, or belonging to, a particular region or environment.

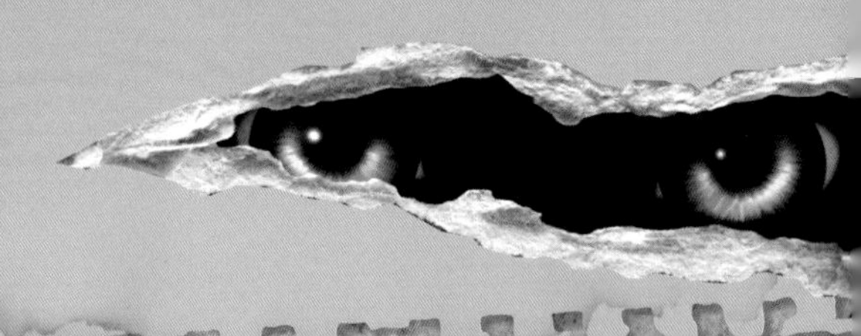

keystone (KEE-stohn) A central stone in a structure, which locks the whole thing together.

loch (LOK) A Scottish lake.

meteors (MEE-tee-orz) Small bodies of matter from outer space that enter Earth's atmosphere.

Moors (MAWZ) North African people who conquered Spain in the eighth century AD.

mythology (mith-OL-oj-ee) A set of stories which are often legendary in nature and feature gods and heroic deeds.

phenomena (fen-OM-eh-nah) Facts or situations that are observed to exist or happen, especially ones whose cause or explanation is uncertain.

pi (PY) The circumference of a circle divided by its diameter (approximately 3.14159).

plate tectonics (playt tek-TONN-iks) A theory in geology, which states that Earth's solid crust and part of the molten material beneath it is divided into moving plates. The plate movements cause activities such as volcanic eruptions and earthquakes.

pulsate (PUL-sayt) A regular, rhythmic brightening and dimming.

sarcophagus (sar-KAH-fuh-gus) A stone coffin.

schooner (SKOO-ner) A type of sailing ship with two or more masts.

scrambled (SKRAM-buld) Ordered (a fighter aircraft) to take off immediately in an emergency.

skeptic (SKEP-tick) A person who doubts something that is claimed to be factual.

sonar (SOH-nahr) A system for detecting objects underwater by emitting sounds and pulses and measuring their return after being reflected.

summer solstice (SUH-mer SOHL-stis) The time when the Sun reaches its highest point in the sky at noon, marked by the longest day. The summer solstice marks the onset of summer.

ufologists (yoo-FO-luh-jists) People who study UFOs.

Vikings (VY-kings) Scandinavian people who raided the coasts of Europe from the 8th to the 11th centuries.

This edition created in 2012 by
Arcturus Publishing Limited, 26/27 Bickels Yard,
151–153 Bermondsey Street, London SE1 3HA

ISBN 978-0-545-47824-3

10 9 8 7 6 5 4 3 2 1   12 13 14 15 16

Printed in Malaysia 106

First Scholastic edition, July 2012

ARCTURUS CREDITS
Author: Oliver Doyle
Editors: Kate Overy and Samantha Williams
Designer: Tania Rösler

PICTURE CREDITS
B. Barber: p. 39 top
Bill Stoneham: p. 77
Boyer: p. 52 bottom left, p. 53 top right
Corbis: Front cover top left and top right, back, p. 2 top left, center left, p. 15 bottom left, p. 24 bottom right, p. 27 bottom right, p. 30–31, p. 35 bottom, p. 36–37, p. 38 bottom, p. 40 bottom right, p. 41 top right, p. 43 top right, p. 44 bottom right, p. 45 bottom, p. 46–47, p. 51 top right, p. 58–59, p. 73 bottom right, p. 78, p. 82 bottom left, p. 88–89
Cryptomundo.com: p. 7
Frank Joseph: p. 80 bottom left, p. 81 bottom right, p. 85 top right, p. 86 bottom right, p. 87 bottom right
Getty: p. 18, p. 49
Idaho State University: p. 8
iStockphoto: p. 2 top right, p. 29 top right, p. 55 bottom right, p. 62 bottom, p. 68, p. 69 top left, p. 71
Mary Evans: p. 15 top right, p. 31 top, p. 32 bottom left, p. 33 top right, p. 34 bottom left
P. Gray: p. 42 bottom left
Photoshot: p. 37 top right, p. 46 bottom left
Shutterstock: Front cover bottom left and bottom right, back cover right, p. 2, p. 3 bottom, p. 4–5, p. 6, p. 14, p. 16, p. 17, p. 21 center, p. 22, p. 23 bottom, p. 25 top right, p. 26–27, p. 28–29, p. 32–33, p. 47 top right, p. 48 bottom, p. 50–51, p. 52–53, p. 54–55, p. 55 top right, p. 56–57, p. 57 center left, p. 60–61, p. 63 bottom, p. 64–65, p. 65 top right, p. 67 top right, p. 69, p. 72–73, p. 74 bottom left, p. 75, p. 77, p. 79, p. 83, p. 84, p. 86–87, p. 89 top left, p. 90–91, p. 91 top right, p. 92–93, p. 93 top, p. 95
Solongo Monkhooroi: p. 26 bottom left
The Comic Stripper: p. 5 right
Topfoto: p. 9 top left, p. 11 top right, p. 12–13
Wikimedia: Back cover left, p. 2 center right, p. 10 bottom left, p. 19 center right, p. 56 bottom right
William Stoneham: p. 13 bottom left